D0986157

# THE HERETIC

### The Templar Chronicles
### Book One

## JOSEPH NASSISE

**Second Edition**

The Heretic © 2003 by Joseph Nassise
Jacket artwork © 2010 Neil Jackson

**Harbinger Books**
**Phoenix, Arizona**

# PROLOGUE

N IALL O'CONNOR WATCHED THOSE AROUND him intently. It was early evening, and the Vienna streets were still crowded, which could make spotting a tail difficult. He was a veteran of this kind of operation, however, and so he took his time, carefully examining his surroundings. When he was certain he hadn't been followed from the museum, he stepped into the phone booth on the corner and shut the Plexiglas door behind him. Ignoring the mounted public telephone, he removed a satellite phone from his pocket and dialed an overseas number from memory.

The phone rang several times before it was picked up. O'Connor could sense someone's presence at the other end, could hear the sound of breathing, but nothing was said, not even hello.

Into that silence, O'Connor said, "It's done."

"And?" The voice was deep and liquid, like water running over gravel.

"The Hofberg object is a fake."

Another long moment of silence. Then, "And the other?"

O'Connor thought back to the long hours he'd spent in the Vatican Basilica; the endless lines, the quiet hope of the faithful, the majestic beauty of the cathedral itself. He'd walked beneath Michelangelo's Dome and examined the pilasters, the four square columns that supported it, paying particular attention to the great statues of the saints - Andrew, Helena, Veronica, and Longinus - that rested in niches within them.

There was power in the cathedral, great power. He'd sensed its ebb and flow as it reacted to the faith of those inside; in some fashion almost every object within the building had glowed with traces of it. Even the statue of St. Peter, its right foot worn smooth after generations of caresses by the faithful, had glistened with the faintest of auras though it wasn't known to be anything more than an ordinary sculpture.

The greatest concentration of power had clearly been beneath the Dome. Three of the four statues that he'd examined had blazed with it, a result of the True Relics each of them contained, relics that were easily discernible to a man of his particular talents.

But the statue of Saint Longinus, the one supposedly containing the remnant of the Holy Lance, had not. It was barren, bereft of the same spark of Divinity that so encased the other statutes and their contents.

"That's a fake, too," he said.

"You're certain?"

"Yes. I'd stake my reputation on it."

"Very well. Return to us, and we will begin the next phase of the operation."

"As you wish."

O'Connor closed his satellite phone, put it back in his pocket, and stepped out of the phone booth. Night had come, the Vienna

2

air grown cold and still. He pulled the collar of his greatcoat closer about his neck, glancing around again as he did so. When he was satisfied that he was still alone, he walked to the end of the street, gazing in contempt at the closed iron gates of the Hofberg palace as he passed. Reaching the intersection, he paused for a moment to light a cigarette, waiting for the traffic signal to change. When it had, he stepped out into the street, confident in the performance of his mission and already dreaming of the ways in which he would spend his exorbitant fee.

The smile of expectation still on his face, he didn't see the city bus surge through the intersection against the light, didn't see the wide front grill bearing down on him until it was far too late.

O'Connor's body bounced off the unyielding surface of the speeding vehicle, flipped high into the air and came crashing back down several yards away. From where he lay broken and twisted in the gutter, his dead eyes stared through the windshield of the vehicle at the empty driver's seat.

Across the Atlantic, in a darkened room, a grey hand reached out in the half-light and finally replaced the phone, severing the connection.

# CHAPTER 1

A S THE SUV TURNED IN through the torn and twisted wrought-iron gates that had once guarded the entrance to the estate, Knight Sergeant Sean Duncan looked out the window at the destruction around him and knew the rumors were true.

The devil had indeed come to Connecticut.

The damaged gates were only the first indication.

The marble statue of the angel that had stood watch over the entrance to the commandery now rested on its back in the middle of the drive, one wing still stretched wide, the other crumbled into fragments a short distance away. Its stone eyes gazed unflinchingly at the sky above as if searching for repentance. In the grass just beyond, a group of knights were laying out the bodies of those who had fallen in defense of the gate, the long rows designed to make it easier for the mortuary team as they sought to identify each corpse. Duncan crossed himself and said a quick prayer for the dead men's souls. Farther on, past the lawn, the still-smoking remains of a Mercedes sat in the cul-de-sac before the manor house, the once-fine leather seats cooked to a crisp and melted across the steel springs beneath.

He'd seen his share of combat; it came with the job, but he'd never heard of a Templar commandery being attacked directly. The Holy Order of the Poor Knights of Christ of the Temple of Solomon, or the Knights Templar as they were once commonly known, existed in secret, away from men's prying eyes. The days when the Order guarded the route to the Holy City had long since passed, the general public was no longer even aware of their existence. Finding the base should have been difficult, assaulting and overwhelming its defenses nearly impossible.

But someone had done both.

According to popular belief, the Templars had been destroyed in the 14th century when the Order was accused of witchcraft and the Pope had burned their Grand Master at the stake for the heresy. In truth, the Order had gone underground, hiding its wealth, disguising its power and managing to remain a viable independent entity right up through the end of the First World War. A treaty with Pius XI was followed by a reversal of their excommunication, and the Templars were reborn as a secret military arm of the Vatican. Their mission: to defend mankind from supernatural threats and enemies.

There were thousands of members worldwide, organized into local commanderies. These in turn were gathered into continental territories, each led by a Preceptor. The Preceptors reported to the Seneschal, who in turn answered to the Order's Grand Master, the individual who governed the entire order from its Scottish base at Rosslynn Castle. While the Order was primarily allowed to run itself, it was still an arm of the Vatican. Over the years the Holy See had appointed three cardinals to interact with the Order's senior leaders to help guide the group along a path that did not conflict with the Pope's wishes.

The commandery in Westport, Connecticut, known as Ravensgate, was one of the largest on the East Coast. Only the Preceptor's headquarters in Newport, Rhode Island, dwarfed it. The grounds consisted of thirty-eight acres of rolling green hills bounded on all sides by woodland, putting their nearest neighbors more than two miles away. The manor house was enormous; forty seven rooms, from the firing range in the basement to a chapel in the north wing.

And now it was in ruins.

The driver pulled to a halt next to the smoldering car, and Duncan stepped cautiously out, his hand on the butt of his weapon. The smell of scorched leather and gasoline washed over him, though the stench of burning flesh he'd expected was mercifully absent. As the rest of his protective detail took up position around the vehicle, Duncan continued to assess the scene. He glanced once more out over the lawn at the work crews and then he turned his attention to the manor house itself.

The damage here was no less extensive. The windows had all been blown out; the odd pieces of glass that remained in their frames reflected the rising sun with little flashes of brilliance here and there, but not a single pane remained intact. The front door was smashed, its splintered pieces still hanging haphazardly in the frame. Bullet holes pockmarked the entryway and surrounding facade. There was a three-foot-long crack in the marble steps leading up to the door. The sight of it made Duncan's blood run cold. The amount of force it must have taken . . .

Despite the destruction, there didn't appear to be any immediate threat, so Duncan passed the signal to the driver in the car behind him. A moment later the rear door opened, and Joshua Michaels, Preceptor for the North Atlantic Region, stepped out.

Duncan was the head of the Preceptor's security detail and ultimately responsible for the man's safety in much the same fashion that the Secret Service watched over and protected the president of the United States. He'd held the post for the last three years; the first for Michaels' predecessor and the last two for Michaels himself. It was a highly respected position and one that gave Duncan significant insight into whatever current matters the Order was involved in.

Right now that meant finding out who, or what, had attacked them so viciously.

The Preceptor had chosen to be on-site for the investigation, and they'd quickly made the trip from Rhode Island. A temporary command center had been set up inside the manor house, and it was from there that Michaels intended to oversee the activity.

Duncan took his position at the Preceptor's side, the rest of the team forming up around them. As one they mounted the steps and entered the manor house. Inside they were immediately met by a group of officers, who led them to a room down the hall. As they walked, one of the local commanders brought the Preceptor up to speed, his low voice the only sound other than the clump of the men's booted feet.

A video-conferencing unit had been assembled in the corner of the command center and, upon arrival, Michaels headed directly to it. A technician activated the link, and a moment later, Cardinal Giovanni's face filled the screen.

"What can you tell me, Joshua?" the older man asked.

"Not much yet, I'm afraid, Your Eminence. As you know, the commandery was attacked at some point during the night. Our best guess puts the event in the neighborhood of 3:00 A.M., though we'll be able to narrow that down some once the mortuary team has had the chance to do its work.

"The intruders breached the gates, then struck directly at the manor house. We've been unable to determine if they were after anything else aside from the destruction of the commandery, but it's still early yet. We should know more as the investigation continues. The site's been secured, and the bodies are being tended to. At this point we've yet to find a single survivor. It's starting to look like we're not going to either. Whoever they were, they were thorough."

The cardinal's response was drowned out as the connection momentarily faltered. The Preceptor simply went on, wanting to get the worst of it out of the way and on the table quickly. "Based on what I've seen and learned so far, I'm going to hand the investigation over to Knight Commander Williams and his team."

The cardinal visibly recoiled from the camera in surprise. "The Heretic? Are you certain that's wise?"

"I am," the Preceptor replied. "He's absolutely ruthless. He can't be bribed, he can't be tempted, and he won't stop until he's discovered who or what is behind this attack. His men are all combat veterans, with the experience and firepower necessary to deal with anything they might uncover, human or otherwise. If the situation is as bad as I'm beginning to believe, I can't think of anyone else I'd rather have leading the investigation."

Listening in, Duncan wasn't so sure he agreed. While Williams was technically a member of the Order, having gone through the investment ceremony just like every other initiate who petitioned for membership, he and his Echo Team unit operated more like freelance operatives than true Knights of the Order. Where members of other units were selected and rotated regularly by the regional leaders, Cade handpicked all of his men, and they stayed with the unit until death or injury forced them out. Where other units answered up the chain of command to the Preceptors, Echo Team reported directly to the Knight Marshal, only two steps removed from the Grand Master himself. They had a reputation for bending the Rule, the laws by which the Order operated, and of occasionally following their own agenda. Rumors swirled around Commander Williams like the tide. He'd been accused of everything from practicing witchcraft to speaking with the dead. He was both feared and revered, depending upon to whom you were talking. His nickname, the Heretic, was a result of that fear and the belief among some that he was nothing but a wolf in sheep's clothing, destined to corrupt the Order from within. Duncan tended to agree with them.

But this wasn't his call to make.

The cardinal's expression clearly showed the dissatisfaction he had with the idea, but like a good general he let his people on the ground make the decisions. Reluctantly, he nodded in agreement. "Very well. Keep me informed of your progress."

"I will. Good night and God bless, Your Eminence."

With a hand raised in blessing, the other man said good-bye and the television screen went dark.

Once the connection had been cut, Duncan didn't hesitate. "With all due respect, sir, I think you are better off putting one of the other teams on this. Williams might be more trouble than he's worth."

The Preceptor turned to face him, shaking his head in disagreement. "I know he can be difficult to work with, Duncan, but it's his very independence that can benefit us here. Whoever did this knew not only the location of the commandery, but also how to take it by surprise. Without, I remind you, a single word of warning escaping to the rest of us. That takes more than overwhelming force, it takes detailed knowledge of who and what they would be facing."

"You believe they had inside knowledge," Duncan said, giving voice to the suspicion that he'd been harboring ever since he'd heard of the attack. "You're bringing in the Heretic because of his lack of political connections then."

"Correct, though that's not my primary reason for using him. I'm convinced that Echo Team is the right choice for the job. They're veterans; they know what they're doing. We're going to need the many years of knowledge and skill that they'll be bringing to the table."

Based on what he'd seen outside, Duncan couldn't argue with that.

"Last I'd heard the team was on a two-week leave. Track down Commander Williams and get him here ASAP."

"Yes, sir."

As Duncan moved to carry out his orders, he wondered just how bad things were going to get.

# CHAPTER 2

W ILLIAMS WAS AT THAT MOMENT in an alley in one of Connecticut's rougher neighborhoods, watching the front of a two-story dwelling just up the street from his position. The smell of garbage from the Dumpster he was using for cover was heavy in the early-evening air, though Cade had gotten used to the stench.

"TOC to all units. You have compromise authority and permission to move to Green. I say again, Green." The bone-mike was pressed securely against his lower jaw, the high-tech device carrying his words clearly to the rest of his team though they were spoken in no more than a whisper.

"Five. . ."

He pictured the assault group sitting in their specially modified Expeditions half a block away, the breaching rams in their laps. He knew they were concentrating on the sequence to come; who gets out first, who hits the door first, how to say "drop your gun" in Spanish.

"Four. . ."

His thoughts jumped to the sniper teams on the adjacent

rooftops, his eyes and ears since this assault began. He knew their preparations intimately, from the way they slid that first bullet into the breach with their fingertips, needing the reassurance of feeling it seat properly, to the thousands and thousands of rounds they'd fired, learning the way the weapons reacted to heat and wind and weather.

"Three. . ."

He knew that his sharpshooters were aligning their bodies with the recoil path of their weapons, pressing their hips against the ground, and spreading their knees shoulder width apart for stability. He knew what it was like to stare through a Unertl ten-power scope at the target, watching, waiting for the moment. He'd been there himself, too many times to count.

"Two. . ."

Discipline was the name of the game, and in Cade's unit, it was the only game being played. The stakes were too high, the consequences too horrible for it to be anything but deadly serious.

"One. . ."

His men took out the two guards standing near the front door from 250 yards away, the impact of their .308 caliber rounds knocking the targets backward into the tall grass on either side of the front stoop with barely a sound. As the bodies hit the ground the Expeditions slammed to a halt out front, the rest of Echo Team swarming the house. The front and back doors fell victim to the breaching rams, flash-bangs quickly following, then Cade's men were inside. Brief, sporadic gunfire reached his ears, then silence.

Cade held his breath.

"Echo-1 to TOC. Structure is clear. Objective is secured."

"Coming in," Cade replied. He would have preferred his

usual position on one of the entry teams. He was the type of commander who led by example, not from the sidelines, and staying behind as tactical operations command had been a test of his patience; but his concern over their target's ability to detect his presence had won out over his need to be involved in the action. The need for stealth was over. Signaling Riley, his second-in-command, Cade emerged from cover and strode briskly forward.

He swept up the steps and entered the house, ignoring the snipers' victims lying in the uncut grass on either side of the porch. As he moved swiftly through the lower floor he passed four other bodies, all young Hispanic males, each lying in a rapidly expanding pool of blood. He had no sympathy for their wasted lives; they were on the wrong side of this conflict, and the unflinching hand of righteousness had finally caught up with them. If anything, he was simply pleased that there were four fewer gangbangers on the city streets. It was the man that his team held captive in the kitchen that truly mattered to Cade. Everything and everyone else beyond that was just a means to an end.

Juan Alvarez was seated in the middle of the room in an old chair, his arms pulled back between the steel posts supporting the seat back and his hands secured together with a set of nylon flex cuffs. Wilson and Ortega stood a few feet to either side of the prisoner, their HK MP5s at the ready and aimed in his direction.

His pistol still in hand but pointed at the floor, Cade crossed the room to stand in front of the prisoner. Alvarez looked as if he had just been roused from sleep; his normally slicked-back hair was in disarray, and all he was wearing was a pair of hastily donned jeans. His usual air of smug superiority was still in place, however.

Cade fully intended to change that.

Alvarez had been under surveillance by Echo Team for the last three weeks. During that time it quickly became clear that the Bridgeport police were correct in their suspicions; Alvarez was indeed the primary conduit for the movement of heroin through Connecticut and into the rest of New England.

Cade didn't care about the drugs.

He wanted Alvarez for a far more personal reason, and he wasted no time getting to the point.

"Where is he?" Cade asked.

The prisoner gave him a look of disdain, and a stream of rapid-fire Spanish poured forth from his mouth. Cade understood enough to know that it was more a commentary on his mother's background than an answer to his question.

Shaking his head in resignation, Cade nodded to Riley.

The larger man stepped forward and gripped the back of the prisoner's chair, holding it tightly.

Cade moved closer, placed the barrel of his pistol against the prisoner's left kneecap, and, without another word, pulled the trigger.

Blood flew.

Alvarez screamed.

Riley held the chair firmly in place against the man's struggles.

Cade waited patiently until the screaming stopped. Then, softly, he said, "I don't have time for this. I asked you a question. I want an answer. Where is the Adversary?"

This time, the answer was in English.

"Drop dead, asshole. I don't know who you're talkin' about."

Expressionless, Cade shot him in the other leg, shattering the man's right kneecap.

Alvarez writhed in agony, his muscles straining against the pain. Riley's arms tensed, but that was the only outward sign of the increased effort he exerted to hold the prisoner securely in place.

Over the wounded man's cries, Cade shouted, "Tell me where he is!"

The prisoner lapsed back into Spanish, cursing his interrogator vehemently; but he did not acknowledge Cade's demand. His blood flowed down his legs and began to pool on the cracked linoleum beneath his feet.

Cade snorted in disgust and motioned Riley out of the way. The sergeant lost no time in following orders.

Cade raised the gun and pointed it at the prisoner's face. "Last chance."

With that, Alvarez went abruptly still. His eyes lost focus, as if listening to a voice no one else could hear, and his face went slack. Out of the corner of his eye Cade caught Riley looking at him quizzically, but he kept his eyes on the prisoner, watching him closely and didn't respond.

Without a change in expression, Alvarez began to shake. His head twisted from side to side erratically as it shuddered atop his neck, darting this way and that like a hyperactive hummingbird. His mouth opened wide, stretching impossibly far. It seemed as if he was screaming, but no sound issued forth. Finally, with a loud pop, his lower jaw dislocated itself.

Cade calmly watched, his gun unwavering from the target.

The shaking intensified, the legs of the chair skipping and bumping against the tiles, leaving little skid marks in the blood pooling beneath Alvarez's feet. A strange squealing sound came from his throat. Alvarez's eyes bulged from their sockets, and blood ran freely from his ears.

Still, Cade stood and waited.

It was only when a widening crack appeared in the center of the prisoner's forehead, a crack that dripped a substance far darker than blood, that Cade reacted.

With a twitch of his trigger finger, he put a bullet through Alvarez's skull.

The prisoner and his chair went over backward to lie still on the blood-stained tiles.

In the silence that followed, no one moved for several long moments as they waited to be certain the thing that had once been Juan Alvarez was good and truly dead, then Cade gave the signal, and the team went instantly into motion. One of the men policed the brass from the floor while another checked to be certain no one had left anything behind that might betray their presence in the house. Thirty seconds later the team was filing out the front door and climbing back into the Expeditions, with Cade and Riley taking open seats in the lead vehicle.

Less than five minutes after entry the team was on its way, leaving behind seven bodies to lie cooling in the darkness.

\* \* \*

Later that night.

He stands alone in the center of the street, in a town that has no name. He has been here before, more than once, but each time the resolution is different, as if the events about to transpire are ordained by the random chance found in the motion of a giant spinning wheel, a cosmic wheel of fortune, and not by the actions he is about to take or has taken before.

*He knows from previous experience that, just a few blocks*

*beyond this one the town suddenly ends, becoming a great plain of nothingness, the landscape an artist's canvas that stands untouched, unwanted.*

*This town has become the center of his universe.*

*Around him, the blackened buildings sag in crumbling heaps, testimony to his previous visits. He wonders what the town will look like a few weeks from now, when the confrontation about to take place has been enacted and re-enacted and reenacted again, until even these ragged shells stand no more. Will the road, like the buildings, be twisted and torn?*

*He does not know.*

*He turns his attention back to the present, for even after all this time, he might learn something new that could lead him to his opponent's true identity.*

*The sky is growing dark, though night is still hours away. Dark grey storm clouds laced with green-and-silver lightning are rolling in from the horizon, like horses running hard to reach the town's limits before the fated confrontation begins. The air is heavy with impending rain and the electrical tension of the coming storm. In the slowly fading afternoon light the shadows around him stretch and move. He learned early on that they can have a life of their own.*

*He avoids them now.*

*The sound of booted feet striking the pavement catches his attention, and he knows he has exhausted his time here. He turns to face the length of the street before him, just in time to see his foe emerge from the crumbled ruins at its end, just as he has emerged each and every time they have encountered one another in this place. It is as if his enemy is always there, silently waiting with infinite patience for him to make his appearance.*

*Pain shoots across his face and through his hands, phantoms of the true sensation that had once coursed through his flesh, from their first meeting in another time and place. Knowing it will not last, he waits the few seconds for the pain to fade. Idly, he wonders, not for the first time, if the pain is caused by his foe or by his own recollection of the suffering he once endured at the enemy's hands.*

*He smiles grimly as the pain fades.*

*A chill wind suddenly rises, stirring the hairs on the back of his neck, and in that wind, he is certain he can hear the soft, sibilant whispers of a thousand lost souls, each and every one crying out to him to provide solace and sanctuary.*

*The voices act as a physical force, pushing him forward from behind, and before he knows it he is striding urgently down the street. His hands clench into fists as he is enveloped with the desire to tear his foe limb from limb with his bare hands. So great is his anger that it makes him forget the other weapons at his disposal in this strange half state of reality.*

*The Adversary, as he has come to call him in the years since their first, life-altering encounter, simply stands in the middle of the street, waiting. The Adversary's features are hidden in the darkness of the hooded cloak that he wears over his form in this place, his mocking laughter echoes clearly off the deserted buildings and carries easily in the silence.*

*The insult only adds fuel to Cade's rage.*

*Just as he draws closer, the scene shifts, wavers, the way a mirage will shimmy in the heat rising from the pavement. For a second it regains its form and in that moment Cade has the opportunity to glimpse the surprise in the other's face, then everything dissolves around him in a dizzying spiral of shifting patterns and unidentified shapes.*

*When the scene solidifies once more, he finds himself*

*standing in a cemetery. Large, carefully sculpted angels adorn the nearest of the gravestones, with only the word Godspeed carved beneath them. Older, more decayed stones decorate the other burial plots nearby, but he is not close enough to see the details etched there.*

*A sense of urgency grips him in its bony fist.*

*It forces him into motion, and he sets off across the lawn, winding in and out between the stones, letting that feeling guide his passage until he sees a small plot set off from the rest by a white picket fence. In the strange twilight, the rails of the fence gleam with the wetness of freshly revealed bone. The coppery tang of blood floats on the night air.*

*As he moves closer he can see that the earth on the other side of the fence has been freshly disturbed. A grave lies open, a gaping hole in the peaceful sea of green grass that surrounds it, filled with a darkness deeper than that of the night sky above. This intrusion of the landscape and of the sanctity of the place draws him closer still, pulling him in toward it the way a fly is coaxed into a spider's web.*

*He stops just short of the small fence and gazes down into the darkness of the grave.*

*Unable to see clearly, he places one hand on the fence and leans forward, straining to get a better look.*

*Something moves down there, a furtive motion.*

*Beneath his hand the fence begins to twist and turn, tumbling him forward toward the darkness of that open grave, just as two eyes gleam hungrily from that inky murk . . .*

Cade awoke in the darkness of his bedroom, his heart pounding and his body slick with cold sweat. He lay still for a moment, gathering his breath, and reached out for the phone in the second before its shrill ring pierced the silence of the bedroom.

"I'm on my way," he said into the receiver, then hung up before the startled novice placing the call could explain the reason for the late-night summons.

He does not need that information.

The dream has already told him everything he needs to know.

# CHAPTER 3

J UST OVER AN HOUR LATER there was a soft knock at the door of the Preceptor's makeshift office.

"Come," said Michaels, without looking up from the report he was reviewing. A moment later the door opened to admit the Heretic.

From his position behind and to the right of the Preceptor, Duncan could see Cade Williams was not a large man, but he was an imposing sight nonetheless. His face was all hard lines and angles, without even a hint of softness. This effect was heightened by the wide band of angry scar tissue that stretched from beneath the eye patch covering his right eye, down across his cheekbone and around behind his ear. He entered the room with a graceful economy of motion but with what also seemed to be an air of caution, as if he were gingerly moving through the world around him.

*Maybe he was*, thought Duncan, as his gaze came to rest on Cade's hands. The flesh-colored gloves were professionally made, and a casual glance would not have betrayed their presence, but Duncan had spent the last several years paying attention to even the tiniest of details in order to keep the Preceptor safe and he did not miss them. The sight forced Duncan to wonder anew at this man's abilities.

Seven years ago Williams had been a highly decorated officer of the Massachusetts State Police, serving on the prestigious Special Tactics and Operations team, first as a sniper and later as team commander. He'd been married to his beautiful wife only five months before disaster struck. A hostage situation had forced him into a confrontation with a supernatural entity that Cade had taken to calling the Adversary. His wife had died as a result, and Cade himself had been severely mauled. He'd lost the sight in his right eye, and the flesh on that side of his face had been so savagely disfigured that plastic surgery hadn't even been considered.

He had gone into seclusion for several months after the incident, avoiding the press and doing his best to come to grips with what had happened. Somehow he'd discovered the Order's existence and successfully petitioned to become a member, claiming that his unique talents could be put to use on its behalf.

Duncan knew it hadn't taken long for Williams to rise through the ranks to his current position as Knight Commander.

It was rumored that Cade had joined the Order with ulterior motives in mind, that he believed the information he gained was the best means of locating and confronting the Adversary, that the Order's goals and objectives were secondary to his own. It was said that he was after one thing and one thing only.

*Revenge.*

In preparing for the meeting Duncan had read the unit's after-action reports, the written summaries turned in after any engagement requiring the use of lethal force. Every one of them showed that Echo Team had been exemplary in the performance of its duties. This, of course, reflected well on the team's leader. Yet, Duncan could read between the lines, could see what the other Commanders thought of Williams.

While Cade flawlessly performed as was expected, those who had used his services were always uneasy doing so. They were happiest when he had completed his mission and was on his way. It was there in the written recommendations, in the seemingly casual comments made when discussing him or his unit.

They were afraid of him.

At its heart, the Order was still an arm of the Church. As such, it believed in the divine province of Man and in the salvation garnered through the grace of the Lord. How a man rumored to be able to walk with the dead and able to read a man's mind simply through touch fit into this picture was difficult to determine. Duncan did not blame the others for their fear.

If everything that was said about him was true, Cade Williams was a man who *should* be feared.

Yet, watching Cade wait patiently the Preceptor to acknowledge him, his one good steel-colored eye taking things in with frank appraisal and seeming not the least bit uncomfortable in the Preceptor's presence, Duncan knew one thing for certain.

Cade Williams had the best chance of succeeding at the job ahead.

Michaels finished with his reading, signed the form, and handed it off to his assistant. He rose and extended his hand in greeting. "Thank you for coming, Knight Commander."

"Sir," replied Cade, shaking the man's hand in return.

This close Duncan could see that the patch over Cade's eye hid the majority of the damage to his face, but the scar tissue that peeked around it gave testimony to the ruin beneath. His wide shoulders and strong physique clearly showed his dedication to remaining at the peak of performance. He was dressed in a black sweater, jeans, and a pair of work boots. His hair, thin and dark, hung to just above his shoulders, loose and unfettered.

"Please, sit down," the Preceptor said, indicating one of the two chairs arranged before his desk.

"I'm fine, sir."

"Suit yourself." The Preceptor turned to his new aide, a short, dark-haired man by the name of Erickson who was filing the just-signed report, and said, "That will be all," and waited for him to leave the room before settling back into his own chair. Duncan remained where he was.

"As you've no doubt heard, this commandery was attacked last night by persons unknown," said the Preceptor. "While we don't know precisely what happened, we do know that every single member of the Order that was on the grounds at the time was slaughtered. Clearly, our people resisted; the evidence of a massive firefight is overwhelming. But that's all we know - they put up resistance, then died, down to the last man.

"Which is where you come in, Commander. I'm assigning Echo Team to find out what happened here. Who attacked us? Why? And more importantly, how did they manage to wipe out an entire complement of our people?"

Cade frowned. "With all due respect, sir, we're a combat unit. Wouldn't it be better to put one of the investigative squads on this? They've got the training and the connections to . . ."

Michaels shook his head, cutting him off. "I'd considered that, but I've decided I want a combat team on this right from the start. Eventually, those conducting the investigation are going to run into whoever is behind the attack and will need combat experience to deal with the situation. With your particular expertise, I think you've got the best chance of determining just what is going on and coming up with a plan to put a stop to it."

Cade stared into the Preceptor's eyes for a long moment without saying anything. He glanced up at Duncan momentarily, returned his attention to Michaels, then reluctantly nodded his agreement.

Michaels went on, but Duncan knew by the man's sudden tension that this was a delicate subject. "You'll also need to replace the missing man in your unit."

Cade's answer was swift. "My team is fine as it is, *sir*." There was an edge of steel in his voice.

Duncan tensed, his hand involuntarily moving to the hilt of his sword. He knew there had been a problem with the last Knight assigned to Williams's team, but the file had lacked any details.

The Preceptor apparently wasn't about to bend on this issue just to keep the Echo Team leader happy, however. "We've been attacked, Williams. I want every unit at full strength, particularly yours. You can either pick another team member, or I'll assign one myself. It's that simple, and I'll allow no argument on the issue."

Duncan fully expected an outburst from Williams and he stood ready to impose himself between the two men.

Cade surprised him, however. Instead of arguing, the team leader simply pointed past the Preceptor at Duncan, and said, "Fine. I'll take him."

Duncan didn't know who was more surprised, himself or the Preceptor.

"He's the head of my security detail, Commander," Michaels objected. "Surely there is someone more suitable. Someone not currently under such heavy assignment."

"Again, with all due respect, sir, I would prefer not to add another team member this soon. If you are forcing me to do so, then it is my right to select the man I want, as the Rule itself outlines. I'll take the sergeant. If he's good enough to guard you, he should be good enough to be on my team."

Trapped by his own logic, the Preceptor had no choice but to agree, much to Duncan's dismay.

## CHAPTER 4

C ADE LEFT THE PRECEPTOR'S OFFICE with his new teammate in tow, only to find the other two members of his command team waiting in the hallway outside. It seemed they'd been summoned by the same industrious initiate as he had. With an assignment of this magnitude ahead of them, he was reminded again how lucky he was to have men of such abilities under his command.

The two men couldn't have been more opposite from each other. Master Sergeant Matthew Riley was tall, black, and generally imposing, with wide muscular shoulders and a clean-shaven head. His usual grim expression seemed to have taken on an additional weight after learning what had happened here the previous evening. Sergeant Nick Olsen, on the other hand, was slim, short, and white, with curling reddish brown hair and the type of smile that had you constantly looking over your shoulder, waiting for the practical joke. Riley was demo and weapons; Olsen, computers and electronics.

They'd been with Cade for several years. If he was the mind of Echo Team, they were its heart and soul. Their courage and dedication had been tested under fire time and time again. He trusted them implicitly.

He quickly filled them in on the details of their new assignment and introduced them to Sergeant Duncan. As he did so, Cade thought about his impulsive decision to use his Sight while in the Preceptor's office and of the resulting flash of Power it had shown centered around the new man's hands. It would be interesting to see how the other men in the unit reacted to Duncan's unique gift when they learned about it.

But they'd deal with that later. For the moment, it was time to get to work.

"All right, here's how we're going to tackle this. Riley, I want you focused on the identity of the attackers. I want to know who they are and how they got inside. Olsen, you're in charge of security. I want this place searched top to bottom. I don't care if the locals have done so already; we're going to do it again, our way. Check the electronic surveillance records from last night, see what you can find. Duncan and I will meet with the medical team and see what we can learn from the bodies." He looked at each of them in turn, waited for their nods of agreement. "The Preceptor's given us carte blanche on this one, so if you need equipment or personnel, don't hesitate to requisition them from the locals. Any questions?"

All three shook their heads.

"All right then. Let's get to it."

\* \* \*

A makeshift mortuary had been set up in one of the gymnasiums, the base infirmary being far too small to handle the number of casualties they were facing. The bodies were laid out in long rows stretching the length of the room, while teams of physicians were moving among them with portable computers, trying to match faces, dental records, and fingerprints against the commandery's personnel records. It was obviously going to be a long and tedious process.

Cade picked a row at random and gave a couple of the bodies a quick, visual inspection. While he was no doctor, he'd seen his share of combat wounds. Bullets and explosives had their own unique signatures and were relatively easy to identify. But to Cade's dismay, nothing here looked familiar, which meant they were up against more than the ordinary.

Once the medical team had finished with a body, a recovery team moved in. It was their job to collect any of the Order's communal property that might still be useful; the arms, armor, and equipment that were routinely issued to each soldier. Personal effects were collected for later distribution to the other men who were close to the deceased, for the majority of the Order's members were without family aside from their brethren. As Cade watched the team gently lift the body he had just examined so they could remove its bulletproof vest, he was struck anew at the sacrifice these men made for the sake of their fellow human beings. Forced to live in secrecy. Without family, without friends. Yet dedicating their lives to protecting the innocent from things no sane man would choose to face.

It was a remarkably lonely life, in many respects.

A life he was too well suited for, it seemed.

"Can I help you?"

A dark-haired man in a white lab coat stood nearby, a questioning look on his face, a look that quickly disappeared when Cade turned to face him.

The other man started, but recovered quickly. "Commander

Williams. Forgive me; I did not recognize you at first."

"My unit's been put in charge of the investigation." Cade jerked a thumb over his shoulder at the rows of the dead. "What can you tell me about them?"

The doctor frowned at the abruptness of the Echo Team commander's request. "I've only just started my examination of the bodies. I can't possibly. . ."

Cade cut him short. "I know you haven't been at it for very long. All I want are your initial impressions. Start with what killed them."

"I'm afraid I can't answer that."

"Why not?" Cade asked. He thought he knew the answer and was just looking to the doctor to confirm his own premise.

He wasn't disappointed.

"So far I haven't found a single bullet wound. Or anything else you might expect in the aftermath of a confrontation with a group of well-trained and well -armed attackers, the kind that would be needed to overwhelm a location like this, for that matter. No bullets or bullet wounds. No knife cuts. No telltale patterns indicating the use of fragmentation grenades, or any modern explosive at all, in fact."

"What?" Duncan asked, incredulous, but Cade simply stared at the doctor, waiting for him to go on.

"I've looked at fourteen bodies so far. Seven had their guts torn out. Four were decapitated. Two seemed to have been killed by a high fall; their bones pulped almost beyond recognition. The last one drowned."

"Drowned?" Cade hadn't expected that last one.

"In the fountain in the courtyard," the doctor replied. "Something tore him up pretty good afterward, but it was the water that killed him."

"So what are you saying, Doc?" Duncan asked.

Cleary unhappy with being put on the spot, but knowing he wasn't going to be left alone until he answered their questions, the doctor sighed, and said, "If I had to take a guess, I'd say that nothing human killed these men."

Exactly what Cade had been expecting.

# CHAPTER 5

W HAT ARE WE STOPPING FOR *this time?* Duncan asked himself, and not for the first time that afternoon. After speaking with the doctor, Cade had ordered up a pair of trikes, and the two of them had set out on an inspection of the estate's perimeter. They'd stopped several times so far. Each time Cade would dismount in order to examine something more closely, and each time Duncan had to wonder why. An unadorned section of outer wall. A clump of bushes. A tree with several broken branches. None of them appeared to have any relevance to the mission at hand, and it wasn't long before Duncan grew impatient with the entire process. He kept his mouth shut, though, unwilling to question his new commander's methods. It would have been different were he in charge, but since he wasn't, there wasn't much he could do but grimace and bear it.

They'd covered roughly two-thirds of the perimeter so far and had just emerged from a dense stand of trees into a small clearing near the edge of the estate. This time, Duncan left his engine idling and refrained from dismounting.

He watched as Cade carefully examined a rough, muddy patch of ground not far from where he'd parked his trike. A small, trickling stream ran nearby and the commander moved over to that next, bending to look at it more closely. The stream was running from the mouth of a metal culvert some ten feet away, a culvert that run underground beneath the commandery's outer wall, placed there to help facilitate runoff during the spring months as the thick winter snow melted and flowed downhill.

Duncan knew from inspecting the plans prior to the Preceptor's arrival that, while the pipe was large enough to admit someone, it narrowed in the middle and was bisected by a mesh barrier that stopped anything larger than a rat from crossing from one end to the other. There was no way the attacking force had penetrated the grounds at that point, and Duncan couldn't imagine what it was the commander found so intriguing.

He watched in amazement as Cade went down on one knee, dipped two fingers into the brackish stream, then brought those fingers to his lips. The gesture was so out-of-place that Duncan finally turned off the engine of his trike, dismounted, and walked to the commander's side.

"What is it?" he asked, crouching to examine the water for himself.

"Not sure yet . . ." Cade said, distractedly. He moved forward, carefully watching the flow of water as it emerged from the culvert. He must have seen something, for he suddenly stepped forward and stuck his head into the pipe's opening.

A second passed.

Two.

Then, "A light! Quickly!"

Duncan jumped to obey. He hustled back to the trikes, pulled a high-powered floodlight from the saddlebags on his own machine, and swiftly returned to Cade's side.

"There's something inside. Something moving," the Commander said, as he took the device, switched it on, and shined it into the depths of the culvert.

Something was jammed about twenty feet inside the pipe.

Something that was too big to make it through the narrowing opening that led to the other side.

Something that wore the red insignia of a Knight of the Order.

They wasted no time in going in after him, whoever he was. Duncan was smaller, so he was chosen to make the extraction while Cade radioed for help. As he lowered himself into a crouch and crawled inside the culvert, flashlight in hand, he could hear the Commander barking orders into the radio.

"I need a medical team and a transportation unit dispatched to the south wall immediately, section 193. Prep the medevac chopper and have the pilot standing by for immediate takeoff. If we need him, he's going to have to move swiftly. Also, get ahold of the forensic team and..."

Duncan tuned him out, concentrating on the task before him. The inside of the pipe smelled strongly of rotting algae, and, beneath it, he could taste the thick scent of blood. He noted that the water beneath his feet was tinged with a slight shade of red. Seeing it, he understood what it was that had caught Cade's attention. He had to give the man credit; he knew he would never have noticed so insignificant a detail from the back of a moving ATV.

He kept the flashlight trained down the length of the pipe ahead of him and, as he got closer, he began to make out more details. The man was crammed into the pipe as far as he could go, his body squeezed into the narrower section ahead of him as if he'd been trying to fit inside and gotten stuck. His face and upper body were hidden from view, but Duncan could see the man's hips and lower legs. The grey jumpsuit he wore was liberally stained with blood. One foot was bare, the boot inexplicably missing.

"Med team's on its way. How are we doing?"

"Almost there," Duncan answered back, squeezing himself forward a few feet more. The tunnel narrowed again, and he was forced to get down on hands and knees, the cold metal above pushing against his back. The water flowed over his hands and around his legs, chilling him further. "Just a few feet more."

His right hand touched the man's boot. He was there.

"Hey? Can you hear me? Are you all right?"

There was no answer.

Duncan swept his light over the other man, trying to assess his condition, but the narrowing scope of the tunnel prevented him from seeing anything. He was simply going to have to haul the man out and hope for the best.

"I'm gonna try to pull him out," he called back to Cade, warning him. He shut off the flashlight, and put it down behind him. It wasn't going to do him any good going backward, and he needed both hands for the job ahead. Reaching out, he grabbed the man by both ankles and started shuffling backward, pulling as he went.

Once they were free of the culvert, they carried him over to a soft patch of thick grass and set him down gently. Cade checked for a pulse, then immediately turned his attention to the man's wounds.

"He's alive, but just barely. Another ten minutes..."

Duncan doubted the young initiate even had that much time left to him. A savage wound ran along the right side of the man's ribcage. The gleam of bone and the softer pink of internal organs could clearly be seen. It looked to Duncan as if something large and remarkably vicious had come along and taken a bite out of the man. Other, smaller wounds were visible on his chest and face, round holes bored into his flesh. He'd already lost a tremendous amount of blood, and a thin stream of it continued to flow out of him as every second passed.

"Where the hell is that emergency team?" Cade cursed, looking around frantically while trying to stem the flow of blood from the man's wounds.

It wasn't working.

Duncan was about to suggest putting the man on the back of his ATV and rushing for the manor house when Cade turned to him, and said, "We're out of time. You're going to have to heal him."

The newest member of Echo Team froze, stunned into immobility. It seemed like ages before he found his voice. "Heal him?" Duncan asked, incredulous.

Unable to take his hands away from the man's wounds lest he bleed to death, Cade could only snarl in frustration at his subordinate. "We don't have time to play games, Duncan. I know you can do it. You can't hide that from me. Quickly now, before it's too late!"

Duncan, however, had no intention of healing the man, fellow knight or not. He didn't know how Cade had discovered the secret he'd kept hidden from the rest of the Order, but he wasn't about to end eleven years of abstinence just because the man told him to do so. Some things were more important than others.

"I don't know what you're talking about!" he snapped back, doing his best to act like he was ignorant of the truth.

Whatever Cade said next was drowned in the sudden growl of

an engine as a four-wheel-drive pickup raced into the clearing and stopped just feet away. The medics were suddenly kneeling beside their fallen comrade, ordering Cade to move aside as they worked frantically to keep the man alive.

They did their best; but in the end, it wasn't enough.

The man's wounds were too grievous, his body had lost too much blood. They worked over him for another five minutes after he'd gone, doing what they could to revive him, but eventually they gave up.

As the medical team loaded up the body and prepared to depart, Commander Williams stepped over to Duncan's side. Cade gripped his shoulder, his fingers digging painfully into the muscles beneath. In a low voice that no one else could hear, he said, "The Enemy didn't kill that man. You did. His death is on your hands."

Duncan watched, dismayed, as his new commander turned away, remounted his ATV, and, gunning the engine, took off through the trees toward the manor house in the distance, leaving him behind with the medical team to contemplate his actions, or lack thereof.

For the first time in the eleven years since he'd made the vow never to use his unearthly ability again, Duncan questioned whether he'd made the right decision.

* * *

They regrouped later that evening in the commandery's great hall: Cade, Riley, Olsen, and Duncan. The rest of Echo Team was officially on stand down, waiting for the senior members to determine an appropriate course of action, but they'd been placed on unofficial standby status by the senior NCOs. It was still too early in the investigation to need them, but that didn't mean it would stay that way.

Duncan was the last to arrive. Cade didn't even turn to look at him as he crossed the room and took a seat at the end of the table near Sergeant Riley.

The meeting immediately got under way. Cade turned to his number two, and asked, "Riley?"

The team's security and demolitions expert had been assigned the task of examining any evidence left behind by the attackers. He unrolled a large blueprint of the facility and its surrounding grounds on the tabletop for the other men to see. Clearing his throat, he said, "I started with the gate." He pointed to the entrance into the compound, the same one they had all driven through several hours earlier. "You've all seen it. Clearly it's how the attackers gained access to the grounds. Considering its condition, my first thought was that they had used explosives, but I was unable to find any blast marks or explosive residue on the gate, the columns, or the road itself. Nor did I find any damage to the gatehouse. My next thought was that they had taken a relatively large vehicle and simply driven through the gate, but the lack of paint residue or clear impact point ruled that out as well." Riley shook his head. "Something came through that gate, something big. That's about all I can tell you right now."

Cade nodded in acknowledgment and gestured for him to continue.

"I left a forensic team at the gate, just in case I missed something, and moved on to the rest of the grounds. There were several areas that showed signs of a confrontation. Here, here, and here," he said, pointing on the map to large grassy areas in front of the main entrances to the manor house. "Prior experience says that the local Knights made a stand before the entrances, giving their brethren inside time to prepare themselves for the assault. I collected blood samples and shell casings from all three locations. The blood was sent to the lab for analysis, though I suspect it won't tell us much other than that it came from our brethren. I examined the bullet casings myself; all of them are our standard issue 9mm ammunition. That leaves us with three options; the attacking force didn't fire a single shot, used the same caliber weapons as our troops, or policed their brass so well that they didn't leave behind even one shell."

Remembering the doctor's comments from earlier that afternoon, Cade suspected the former. "Tire tracks? Shoe prints?"

"Neither. If it wasn't for that damn gate, at this point I'd be willing to believe that they flew in over the wall and flew out again the same way, without ever touching the ground. According to the physical evidence, our guys were the only ones here."

Cade turned to Olsen. "What about you?"

"I'm afraid what I have isn't much better. Using some of the Preceptor's men, I organized search parties to cover the entire estate, particularly the manor house. We searched this place top to bottom. We looked in every room, every closet, every nook and cranny. Except for the wounded man you and Duncan discovered, we didn't find a single survivor. It's really too bad the medics weren't able to save him; we might have learned something from him. Right now, all we've got is a lot of bodies and no answers."

Duncan waited for Williams to denounce him in front of the other squad members, but the Commander simply nodded at Olsen to continue.

"While the teams were searching the grounds, I spent some time checking the electronic infrastructure. The alarms and emergency warning systems are all functional. So are the cameras. Yet last night, every single one of them failed for approximately three and a half hours for no known reason. The backup systems also went down." Olsen looked at each of them. "Whoever they were, they came through our security like it wasn't even there. They knew exactly what defenses we had in place. Even worse, they knew just how to get around them."

Duncan didn't like what that implied. It added more credence to the Preceptor's belief that it had been an inside job, something Duncan would have considered inconceivable before then.

For the first time, Cade looked in his direction. "Where did we get with the interviews?"

Duncan met his gaze squarely. Was that a flash of contempt in his eyes? *No matter, concentrate on the business at hand,* he thought. After he'd escorted the med team back to the manor house, he'd been ordered to interview the men who'd first discovered the situation. "I confirmed that the men had been isolated from each other since our arrival, and then interviewed them one at a time. Aside from a couple of insignificant details, they tell the same basic story." Duncan knew the other team members would be measuring his response, trying to get a sense for how he would fit into the group. He spoke calmly, carefully weighing his words, directing his response to Cade but knowing the other two sergeants were listening as well. First impressions were important.

"Both men had been on leave together, rock climbing in New Hampshire for the weekend. They received an urgent page from the duty commander at around 3 A.M. this morning, signaling them to return as soon as possible. They packed their gear and drove south immediately thereafter, arriving here around 7 A.M. They were obviously too late."

Duncan glanced down at his notes, before continuing. "I checked their service records; they both seem to be good men, dedicated to the Order and to its mission. They are clearly distraught over what has happened, and so far haven't given me any reason to distrust their explanation or question their story." Finished with his report, he sat back and waited.

"All right," said the commander, after only a few moments of thought. "Unless forensics comes up with an angle we haven't seen yet, we're going to have to do this the old-fashioned way. I want all three of you working the files first thing in the morning. Start with the latest threat assessments. I want to know every single individual or organization in the last six months that has been labeled by our intelligence people as dangerous. Of those who have actually made threats against us, I want to know who has the manpower, financing, and equipment to pull off an assault like this one. After that, we need a list of any other group or groups that are capable of such an attack, regardless of whether they've showed up on a recent watch list or not." His gaze swept the table and the men seated around it. "They caught us once unprepared. That will have boosted their confidence. Chances are they'll hit us again. The longer we take to get a lock on who they are, the higher the likelihood of its happening again."

Cade turned to face Riley. "I'm going to recommend to the Preceptor that he place all of the North American commanderies on alert effective immediately. I want you to work with the temporary base commander to come up with a suitable way of protecting this location in case they decide to take another shot at us this evening. When you're done with that, put the rest of Echo on twelve-hour standby."

"I have the feeling we're going to need them sooner rather than later." With that final comment hanging in the air, the commander stood, indicating the meeting was adjourned.

# CHAPTER 6

EMPLETON COMMANDERY, CINCINNATI, OHIO.

Knight Lieutenant Nathan Jessup stared nervously out into the fog.

Unusually thick and heavy fog.

Instead of clinging to the ground in small, swirling pools and eddies, it rose like a wall, sweeping down the length of the road that was the only entrance to the estate, a juggernaut inexorably marching forward. From where he stood on the opposite side of the tall iron gate that governed access to the property from the road, Jessup watched the fog advance slowly through the night until it stopped a few hundred feet from the gate.

He shivered, and not as a result of the cold September night air. He turned away from the sight and stepped back inside his guard shack. He crossed to the small portable heater and stood in front of it, trying to warm the chill from his bones.

Every few moments, however, his gaze was drawn back to the windows and the slowly advancing fog that crept its way toward him and his meager sanctuary.

Ordinarily he didn't mind such weather. It made driving some of the backcountry roads a bit difficult and played havoc with his ability to keep his window clear, but that was usually the worst of it.

This fog was different, though. Its very presence tugged at his nerves, and, more than once, Jessup felt like someone was watching him when his back was turned.

Watching.

Waiting.

Moving closer.

He shook off the uncomfortable feeling and decided he'd stood there alone in the dark long enough. It was time to hear another human voice and remember he wasn't the only one out on the grounds pulling guard duty that night. He put the handheld radio close to his mouth, intending to check in with control, when a sound from out beyond the gates reached his ears. Lowering his hand before keying the mike, he stepped outside his guard shack to investigate.

A minute passed with Jessup standing just inside the gate, his head cocked to the side in an effort to hear better.

Two minutes.

Three.

He was about to give up and blame it on his overactive imagination when he heard it again

From out of the fog came the sound of human footsteps, muted by the damp air, but audible nonetheless.

As Jessup listened, the footsteps grew closer.

Gradually, a figure could be seen, moving out of the haze toward the gates. It was indistinct at first, nothing more than a darker stain against the lighter fog where the spotlights cut into its heart, but before long, as it grew closer, Jessup could tell it was a man.

Whoever he was, he was dressed against the night's chill in a long overcoat with a hood pulled up and over his head, obscuring his face from view. The boots on his feet struck the pavement with hard, sharp footfalls, clearer now that he had emerged from the fog, the sound following each step like a devoted puppy.

The visitor strode up to the gate and stopped.

Jessup watched the man examine the gate, him, and the area beyond, but the man's hood shrouded his face in darkness, and the guard was unable to see his features.

"Can I help you?" asked Jessup.

His own voice sounded strange to his ears, the fog muting the sound and making it seem flat and lifeless.

The visitor made no response.

Jessup stepped a few feet closer, the radio in his right hand forgotten, his left hand on the butt of the pistol at his waist. "Sir? This is private property. Can I help you with something?"

A strange sound came from the dark depths of that hood in response. It took Jessup a moment to realize what it was.

Sniffing.

The man was sniffing the air, like a dog tracking a scent. His head moved in a slow circle, the sniffing continuing, until at last it came to rest pointed about fifteen degrees off center.

Turning his head to follow, Jessup realized that the manor house lay directly through the trees in that direction, despite the fact that it couldn't be seen from the street.

Jessup felt his skin crawl at the sight, and a chill passed through him. He'd had enough; this was just too weird. Turning back to his mysterious visitor, he opened his mouth to order him away from the property.

The words never left his throat.

When he turned around he found that the fog had suddenly

jumped forward, closing those last few hundred feet until it stood like a barrier on the heels of his hooded visitor. It writhed and rolled, churning about like it had a life of its own. Faces could be seen here and there within its depths, grey distorted shapes with mouths open wide in silent screams, ghostly phantoms shrieking for release.

Jessup stumbled backward, the radio falling from his right hand in shock as his left hand clawed frantically for his weapon.

He was too late.

The intruder raised an arm and pointed a hand at the gate, a hand that was battleship grey in color, with an extended finger tipped with a long, curving, yellow nail. A high-pitched keening suddenly burst from inside the thing's hood.

The sound was deafening in volume, pounding at Jessup's ears, forcing all thoughts out of his head except the need to cover his ears and escape from the noise. He forgot both the radio and the gun, slipping to his knees and using his hands to try and block out the sound. Despite this, he found he couldn't take his eyes off the figure standing on the other side of the gate.

The fog grew more agitated as the keening continued, the faces forming and dissolving at a furious speed, each more horrible than the last. Then something larger moved with the depths of the fog.

Jessup watched in horror as the fog suddenly charged the gate. He glimpsed an indistinct shape of horrendous proportions in its depths, then the bars of the gate were peeled apart to create an opening large enough for a man.

The strange visitor stepped through the gate, chuckling to himself, and the fog followed obediently at his heels.

The sound of Jessup's screams soon drowned out the newcomer's laughter.

\* \* \*

The battle was going well, so much so that the man born as Simon Hamilton Logan but now known to his followers simply as the Necromancer decided it was time for phase two. He and his acolytes changed their clothing and swiftly climbed inside the two vans that would take them to the other side of the commandery grounds, where a small cemetery awaited their attention.

The driver in the lead van parked behind a small grove of trees to the left of the cemetery, shielding it from the manor house that served as the commandery's main operations center. The other parked just behind the first. Eight figures emerged from the vehicles, all of them dressed in the same dark robes. Two reached back into the rear vehicle and dragged out a young woman, her hands bound behind her back and a gag in her mouth. The drugs they'd given to her made her docile, but also required that she be supported on either side in order to walk. A few of the men carried shovels. Two of them lugged large duffel bags over their shoulders while another led a young black Labrador on a leash. Logan was attired in a similar manner as the others, though his robe was made of finer materials and it had a number of Kabalistic symbols sewn into it in gold thread.

He listened for a moment to the sounds of combat drifting through the night air from the direction of the manor house and smiled in satisfaction. All was going according to plan.

He gave the signal, and the group moved out among the gravestones, their flashlights briefly illuminating the face of each marker before moving on to the next, obviously seeking one in particular. With eight of them looking, it took less than ten minutes.

While those with the shovels went to work on the grave, piling the dirt beside the headstone, two others began to lay out large circles made of salt from the supplies drawn out of the duffel bags, one circle around the grave itself and another several yards away on a bare patch of earth. Each circle was precisely nine feet in diameter, and both were left temporarily incomplete.

Logan stood to one side, watching. When things were ready he gave the command for the dog to be brought forward and placed inside the second circle, where it was laid on its side on the ground and its legs tied together. The drugs it had been given earlier kept the dog docile and quiet, despite the restraints.

The diggers reached the coffin. One of them climbed out of the open grave and helped the circle-makers erect a block and tackle set over it. The loose ends of the rope were thrown down to those below and secured around the coffin they had just unearthed. Five minutes later it was raised high enough to be dragged over the lip of the pit and settled on the ground beside it, well within the circumference of the salt circle. One man stepped forward and, with a small hammer and chisel, smashed the latches that held the black-lacquered lid closed.

Logan smiled with satisfaction.

It was time for the ritual to begin.

The woman was brought forward and deposited next to the casket, where one of the men knelt to tie her feet. Her drugged senses barely registered the change.

As the rest of the men stepped away from the casket and moved to stand behind the smaller circle several yards away, one of them took up a handful of salt and closed the circle that now surrounded the casket and the woman. He then rejoined the others, sealing the entire group inside a circle of their own.

The use of the circle as a protective barrier was as ancient as the practice of magick itself. Once activated with the appropriate incantation, the salt barrier would withstand even a direct attack by an inhabitant of the lower planes and should easily protect the Council members from the revenant the Necromancer intended to raise. While the circle around the coffin itself should keep the revenant safely trapped behind its barrier, redundancy was a tactic only ignored by the foolish when performing magick of this caliber, hence the additional circles around the participants themselves.

Logan used more of the salt to draw a series of Sumerian symbols around the inner circumference of the circle, symbols that a month ago he hadn't known even existed.

When he was finished, he used the small remaining portion of salt to close the circle behind him, sealing himself, his assistant, and the dog inside its protective barrier.

The assistant readied the rest of the equipment; set up a small folding table, covered it with a swath of fine silk, and arranged the bowls and the obsidian athame, or ritual knife, in the necessary sequence. The dog was next. It was tied down to the tabletop, its legs stretched in both directions, leaving its belly exposed. As the other man worked, the Necromancer considered the rite he was about to perform, a rite that, without the tutelage of the Other, he never would have been powerful enough to handle. Nor would he have had the aid of the men around him, men who had been seduced by his connection to the demonic and joined him in forming the Council of Nine. Yet the Other needed them as well, needed human servants to carry out those tasks that it was prevented from handling on its own, like invading the holy ground of a Templar commandery. It was a partnership made of a mutual desire and greed for power, one that the Logan fully understood and encouraged. When it was all said and done, he would be that much more powerful, more capable of carrying out his own plans of conquest.

For him, power was the ultimate reward.

Now that he had it, he knew that he would do anything to keep it.

*Anything.*

He stepped over to the table. The assistant had finished with the necessary preparations, having added two golden bowls, an incense burner, and a variety of herbs to what was already on the table.

As his assistant set a heady combination of belladonna, mandrake, henbane, and opium burning in the incense dish, the rest of the Council began to chant. The chanting started softly at first, a low, sonorous drone, that gradually built in volume and timbre until it became a strange, high-pitched keening that picked at the nerves. The sound rose and fell, fell and rose, dancing along the wind's edge like a bird of prey.

An electrical tension filled the air, similar to that felt before a summer storm, yet what was looming was far less benign than such a simple act of nature. A wind kicked up suddenly, sliding amongst the gravestones, hissing in sibilant whispers as it grew in strength, setting the ends of the Council members' robes fluttering in its breeze.

When the song was at its height, the wind howling around him as if in counterpoint, Logan raised the obsidian knife high over his head.

With one sudden, downward swing, he slashed the canine's throat.

Blood flowed, hot and wet in the night air.

The assistant stepped in with the smaller of the two bowls,

catching the streaming liquid.

Logan used his knife again, this time on the dog's exposed stomach, slashing it open from stem to stern, working quickly so that he could complete the ritual before the dog died. Setting the knife down on the table, he turned back and plunged his hands inside the still-warm carcass, drawing forth handfuls of entrails. These he smeared liberally about his face and neck, breathing in the thick scent of death and the coppery smell of freshly spilled blood, using the physical senses to activate his arcane ones, linking him with the realm of the dead.

With a snap, power suddenly flooded through his body, and he grinned at the sheer thrill of wielding such might.

He felt it coalesce in the air around him like a living, breathing creature, and with a sharp thrust of both his arms, he flung it outward to strike the exposed coffin.

Logan laughed aloud, heady with power.

* * *

Templar Knights Stan Gibson and Neil Jones had been separated from their unit in the confusion of the surprise assault on the commandery and found themselves wandering on the outer periphery of the battle.

"What is that?"

Gibson turned his head and glanced toward where his partner was pointing. Across the lawn near the old cemetery, a bright glow of greenish -colored light could be seen playing across the grounds.

Curiosity got the better of them.

Moving carefully and staying in the trees as much as possible, the knights crossed the distance to the cemetery. They approached the gates slowly, using hand signals to inform each other of their intentions. Jones slipped through the gate first while Gibson covered him with the shotgun before following behind.

They could hear voices, chanting in a strange tongue, the sound rising and falling with the wind like some insane chorus, causing the hair on their arms and the backs of their necks to stand at attention.

Cautiously, they moved closer.

\* \* \*

Surprisingly, the spirit he was calling forth fought back with a power almost equal to his own.

Logan could feel the spirit resisting his call to return to its former body, fighting his commands to cross the barrier and answer his summons. Frustrated, the necromancer increased his efforts.

It quickly became a battle of wills, Logan's arcane power pitted against the righteous nature and faith of the former Templar Knight, each side refusing to give in. Power spit and crackled inside each of the circles like hot grease on a grill, and the smell of burning ozone filled the air. The Council chanted, the Necromancer forced more of his power back down the link that connected him to the shade, and still the knight sought to avoid being called from his rest for so nefarious a purpose.

As a result, the energy began to spill over, no longer affecting just the target grave but those in the immediate vicinity as well, seeping down into the earth to affect coffins on all sides. Where the bodies inside them were too decayed to support their return, the indistinct forms of apparitions began to appear, hovering over their gravestones or rising slowly out of the ground. Their lack of physical form fueled both their hunger for life and their anger at the living. When mixed with the Necromancer's potent magick, they became not ghosts but spectres, vile creatures with a desire and craving to bring harm to the living.

There were hundreds of them, and the cemetery grounds gave birth to more and more, swelling their ranks, as the Necromancer continued to pour more and more energy into the confrontation.

The Council ignored the presence of the spectres, knowing they'd be safe locked within their protective circle.

In counterpoint to the Council's chanting, the ghosts took up an unearthly screeching of their own, warbling and weaving in syncopation.

At that moment, Gibson and Jones appeared from out of the darkness and walked into full view of the necromancer, the Council, and the spectres.

Nothing they had been taught could ever have prepared them for the sight.

* * *

"Freeze!" Gibson cried out, as they stepped into view. The muzzle of his gun was locked on the tall figure off to his right, which seemed to be the source of the green light.

"Mary, Mother of God" Jones whispered.

Following his partner's gaze, Gibson looked to his left.

The dead stared back at him.

A young man stood just a few feet away, one side of his head crushed like an aluminum can, his eyes bulging from the pressure. Nearby stood another man, the whiteness of his bones gleaming through his decomposing flesh. There were hundreds more of them; some nearly perfect, so that you wouldn't have known they were dead if you'd passed them on the street, some so corrupt and decayed that they were barely recognizable as human.

Some they knew.

Around them hovered those phantoms that had returned from the other side only to find that their bodies could no longer contain them. These wraiths were less distinct, flashes of ghostly luminescence that flickered in and out of existence. Gibson could see that their faces were strangely distorted, as though they had been twisted and pulled in different directions at once. They stared out at him through dark, eyeless sockets, and from out of their mouths came a high pitched screaming.

For a moment, no one moved.

Then the dead came at them in a rush.

Gibson and Jones opened fire.

They might as well have been whistling "Dixie" for all the good it did them.

Gibson's shotgun knocked several of the revenants off their feet with its sheer power, but those behind simply charged forward over the bodies of their brethren without hesitation even as those that had fallen struggled to get back to their feet. The spectres were immune to the officer's bullets and quickly swarmed forward.

"Get back!" Jones yelled, and Gibson nodded his understanding, though he could barely hear him over the sound of the dead. The two men turned to run, only to find that the dead were on all sides.

The end came quickly.

Something spectral clawed at Gibson's face, opening a large furrow in his cheek, while at the same time a sudden pain flared in his leg. He looked down to find a revenant with its rotting teeth clamped around his ankle. When he lowered the shotgun to blast the creature into obscurity, others rushed forward, grasping at him.

Gibson went down in a pile of bodies, his screams rising to join those of the dead.

Jones's pistol went silent at that point as he used up the last of the ammunition he was carrying. He hurled it at the face of the first revenant that got close enough, then stuck out with his fists and feet, as the dead swarmed over him.

* * *

The spectacle over, the Necromancer turned his attention back to his task. He could feel the spirit weakening, could feel the struggle shifting in his favor, so he reached down for his reserves and poured more energy into the fray.

And won the struggle.

A moment later the lid of the coffin was thrown violently open from the inside.

A hand, spotted with mold, was thrust up into the night air.

"Arise!" the Necromancer commanded, and the revenant inside the casket obeyed, forcing itself upright to stand on wobbly legs.

As it stepped clear of the casket, its gaze fell upon the woman lying bound and gagged at its feet.

With a cry of both anguish and hunger, the creature threw itself upon the offering and began to feed.

Logan laughed aloud at the sight, uncaring.

# CHAPTER 7

THEY WERE AWOKEN BEFORE DAWN with the report of another attack, this time in Ohio. Less than twenty minutes after being informed of this new development, Echo Team was airborne, headed for the site of the latest confrontation. Driven to the airport by the same novice who'd delivered the note, they found one of the Order's Gulfstream IV aircraft waiting for them, courtesy of the Preceptor. Within moments of their arrival the group boarded the plane and took off.

Like most of the Order's equipment, the interior of the aircraft was partan. Gone were the leather seats and the recessed minibars, the inflight entertainment centers, and the four-star meals. Only the bare necessities had been spared, though the privacy curtain that separated the main compartment from the smaller, private compartment to the rear remained.

Riley was up front with the pilot. Duncan was seated in the middle compartment with Olsen, who had spent the time since boarding searching through a variety of databases on his laptop. He hadn't yet said a word to his new teammate, so Duncan was surprised when Olsen suddenly sat back and asked, "So what's your story?"

Duncan looked up from the magazine he was idly flipping through and across the aisle to where the other man was seated. "My story?"

Olsen was older than Duncan, though not by more than a few years. He carried himself with the assured confidence of a man who had seen and conquered all that life had thrown in his path. His rust-colored hair was cut short in military fashion, and his beard was trimmed so that it neatly framed his narrow face.

"Yeah, you know, where you're from, why you joined this crazy outfit in the first place?" The other man acted casual, but Duncan knew there was more than idle interest in the question.

"Not much to tell," Duncan replied. "I was born and raised in Georgia. Undergrad and grad degrees in religious studies, then spent some time in the missionary field before being asked to join the Order."

"Missionary work, huh? Where?"

"Mostly in Southeast Asia. Thailand, Laos, even spent about six months in mainland China." *And I hope I never set foot in that country again*, he thought grimly, the events that had led him to the Order still fresh in his mind even after all this time.

Nick must have picked up on his discomfort, for he didn't pursue that point further. "How long have you been in?" he asked.

"Ten years. Three in the general forces and the last seven on the protection detail for the Preceptor. I've seen my share of things get ugly, but I'll be the first to admit it pales in comparison to Echo Team's exploits. From the unit's record, you seem to see combat fairly often."

Nick smiled, and it was not a friendly smile. "You bet your

ass we do. More than any other unit. When the higher-ups can't figure out how to solve something, they call us in. This new job might seem quiet now; but I guarantee it's going to get sticky, or we wouldn't be here."

"Can I ask you something then?" Duncan inquired.

Nick opened his mouth but before he could reply his laptop beeped. Muttering under his breath, he began to tap the keyboard with sure, quick strokes. "Go ahead, I'm still listening," he said to Duncan, without taking his eyes off the screen.

Duncan nodded toward the rear of the aircraft and asked, "How do you feel about working for him?"

Nick stopped what he was doing and eyed Duncan in silence. Just as Duncan began to suspect that he had crossed a line he shouldn't have crossed, the other man finally answered. "What you really mean is what's it like working for the Heretic, right?"

Duncan grimaced at his transparency, but nodded nonetheless. "Well, he does have a certain reputation."

Nick snorted. "Let me give you a piece of advice. If you're going to be a part of this squad, then you need to get something straight, and it's best that you do it from the start," he said, the casual air now gone from his voice. "In our unit, no one ever calls Cade the Heretic. It's a bullshit name given to him by someone not even fit to be in the same room with him. You'll understand that the first time you find yourself facing something that belongs inside someone else's nightmare, and it's Cade that saves your ass."

Nick laughed suddenly at his own harshness and softened his tone. "I'm not trying to be hard on you. Even I have to admit that things are a little, um, different on the team. Cade doesn't always follow the Rule precisely to the letter, and he has certain abilities that, frankly, scare the hell out of me sometimes. But that doesn't mean I don't respect him or that he doesn't deserve my respect. He's the best damn commanding officer I've ever served under, that's a fact."

"So the stories are true?" Duncan asked.

"That depends on which ones you are talking about," Nick answered, with a sly smile.

* * *

From his position at his work area in the rear cabin, Cade could hear the soft hum of conversation between Sergeant Olsen and their new team member, reminding him that he had yet to go over the man's personnel file.

With a sigh he turned away from his research in the *Apostolicæ Sedis* and opened his laptop. Powering it up, he called forth Duncan's service records.

He skimmed over the early details - born and raised in Georgia, the son of a preacher, home schooled for most of his elementary years, attended a parochial high school and later a Jesuit university, where he majored in religious studies - it was all fairly ordinary. Instead, Cade focused on the present, noting the short span of time Duncan spent in seminary before an unexpected departure for the Orient and a long missionary tour, then the equally short courtship to bring him into the Order. His zeal and desire to succeed once he had been christened a Knight was evident, and his service record over the last ten years was exemplary. He'd been selected early on to serve on the protection detail and had remained there, rising to his present position as detail command three years ago.

A series of photographs were included as scanned images embedded into the report, and Cade took the time to study each of them in turn, hunting for evidence that his hunch had been right, that the flash of Power he'd seen centered on Duncan's hands in the Preceptor's office was an earthly indicator of his ability to heal with just a touch.

He stopped to look more closely at one of the older photographs. The image was creased and worn; whoever had scanned the photo did not bother to clean it up. It was clear enough, however, to show a young Sean Duncan standing unhappily in front of an older man dressed in a suit. Duncan looked to be around ten or eleven years old. The man, looking stern and serious, rested his hands on young Sean's shoulders. The pair stood beneath the entrance to a revivalist tent, the sign marking the doorway partially obscured by the older man's arm.

**Special Engagement**
**Tonight and tonight only**
**Pastor Patrick Duncan**
**Faith Hea . . . .**

*Now we're getting somewhere,* thought Cade.

He printed a hard copy of the photo and settled back in his chair, staring at the photo as if it might suddenly reveal some long-lost secret that only Cade would understand.

Perhaps, in a way, it did.

\* \* \*

Duncan was startled out of a light sleep by a hand on his shoulder.

It was Nick. "Boss wants to see you," he said, gesturing to the smaller cabin at the back of the plane, where Cade had been sequestered since the fight began.

Nick returned to his seat. Duncan unbuckled his seat belt, walked down the aisle, and drew aside the curtain hanging at the end of the forward cabin.

The lights were on low but provided enough illumination that Duncan could see the area served as a functional work space. The standard aircraft seats, like those in the forward cabin, had been taken out. In their places were two reclining chairs with a table between them and a large drafting-style worktable. The lights were on over the worktable, shining down on several stacks of papers, a few open reference books, and a long black case.

Williams was nowhere in sight.

Noting that the lavatory lights on the rear wall were illuminated, Duncan guessed that Cade would be back momentarily. His curiosity getting the better of him, he made his way over to the worktable.

The books were old, centuries so, if the fine calligraphic script and the carefully drawn illustrations in the margins were any indication. A glance at the text revealed it to be Latin, a confirmation of the authenticity and age of the volumes. Judging by the images and the few snatches of text he quickly translated, each of the books dealt in some fashion with angels and demons.

His personnel file lay closed on the table nearby.

Resisting the urge to peek inside it, he turned his attention instead to the long, narrow case that rested on the table beside them.

It was a sword case. Duncan had no difficulty identifying it, for he had one of his own; every Knight in the Order did. They were given out by the Seneschal during investment ceremonies, a symbol of the oath of fealty that each man gave as he joined the Order.

But Cade's was different.

Where Duncan's case was made from simple black fiberglass without ornamentation, Cade's was covered with a soft supple skin of dark leather and held shut with three simple silver clasps. In the center of the lid, a word had been branded into the covering, its harsh, rough edges providing a stark contrast to the rest of the case's beauty.

The word was in a language Duncan did not recognize.

Duncan glanced up at the lavatory lights, saw that they were still lit, and gave in to a sudden impulse. He reached down and opened the case.

Inside, lying on a bed of smooth, white silk was Cade's sword, as Duncan had expected.

The weapon itself was an unadorned English longsword. Along the length of the blade that was facing upright in the case, the word *Defensor* had been inscribed in silver.

Latin again and easily identifiable to Duncan.

Translated, it meant Defender. It was etched into every sword carried by the Templars, for that one word neatly formed the foundation of the Order's mission – to defend mankind against the evils in the world.

Awed by the beauty and craftsmanship that went into creating this particular weapon, Duncan couldn't resist. He reached down and carefully withdrew the sword from the case. He held it up in the aisle, turning it slightly to and fro so that the dim lighting of the cabin made the script sparkle and shine.

Doing so, he noted something else.

On the opposite side of the blade, a second word had been inscribed, in a fashion similar to the first.

*Ulciscor.*

Vengeance.

Seeing it made Duncan pause, both for its very presence and what it said about the weapon's owner. According to the Code, a Knight was allowed personal ownership of only a few, specific items. The sword given to each of them during the investiture ceremony was one of them, a symbol of their fidelity to the Order and their unrelenting dedication to its ideals. The weapons were supposed to remain undecorated, chaste, if you will. Enhancing the weapon in any manner after it is awarded is cause for a variety of punishments, for doing so is considered a sin of pride.

Duncan's new commanding officer had clearly ignored this aspect of the Rule.

*How many others does he ignore?*

He didn't have time to ponder the answer.

"Like it?" a gruff voice asked from the darkness at the rear of the cabin, startling the younger knight and almost causing him to drop the weapon in surprise as he looked up to find his new commander leaning against the door of the lavatory, watching him.

Embarrassed to be caught, Duncan mumbled an apology beneath his breath and quickly replaced the sword in its case. Cade moved farther into the cabin and took a seat in one of the reclining chairs, gesturing with one gloved hand for Duncan to do the same.

"Tell me about your gift," Cade said.

Duncan started, clearly expecting to be taken to task for his transgression and unprepared for the question. "What?"

Duncan's eyes followed Cade's gloved hands as his new commander reached up and removed his eye patch.

"Could you heal this?" Cade asked.

Duncan stared.

He was unable to look away. The destruction to the right side of Cade's face was worse than Duncan had expected. It appeared as if someone had taken a blowtorch to the tender flesh around his eye socket, the skin flowing and surging together in a grotesque parody of the natural order of things. The eye itself was still intact, but was nothing more than a milky white orb floating in a sea of damaged flesh.

"Good Lord," Duncan breathed.

His hands drifted up from his lap toward Cade's ruined face, seemingly of their own accord, but he snatched them down again as soon as he realized they were in motion.

Duncan glanced away, unable to continue to meet his commander's gaze. When he again found his voice, he replied, "No. No, I couldn't heal that."

"Why not?" Cade asked, making no move to cover his face or lean back out of the light.

Duncan shook his head in frustration. "It's too old. I can only heal things that are fresh. Tissue that hasn't scarred over." He stared at his hands, not for the first time cursing their limitations. Without looking up, he said to Cade, "I'm sorry."

"Don't be," came the reply, and to his amazement Duncan heard humor in Cade's voice.

"I'm long since over it. I was more interested in your reaction than anything else."

"You were testing me," Duncan said matter-of-factly.

"Of course," Cade replied, nodding. Referring to the other man's ability, he asked, "Does the Order know?"

"It's not general knowledge, but it's probably in my file somewhere," Duncan replied.

"Have you tested its limits?"

Duncan's mind swept back over the years spent overseas, the endless lines of the sick and the injured, the bright sparkle of hope in their faces, their utter belief that he and he alone could heal them of their afflictions. Wearily, he said, "Yes. I've tested it."

Cade nodded but didn't push him any further, for which Duncan was grateful.

"I suspect that you are going to learn a lot in the next few months," Cade told him. "Things that you will probably wish you had never learned. You'll see things the ordinary man will most likely never see, but that is one of the crosses that we bear in service to the Order. I'll expect you to do your duty no matter what the situation. If you can do that, you'll have the respect of every man in this unit. Understood?"

Duncan nodded.

Cade continued, "You've probably heard a lot about me – some good, some bad, I'll wager. I won't comment on any of that except to say that I'll expect you to make up your own mind. Like you, I have certain abilities, abilities that not everyone understands. Sometimes I'm forced to use them in ways others would consider unconventional. But I took the same oath to the Order as you did. Remember that.

"As you know, Echo Team is made up of four squads plus a command unit. Martinez is in charge of First Squad, Wilson has Second, Baker and Lyons have Third and Fourth Squad respectively." Cade continued by spending several minutes going over the standard operating procedures in the unit; hand signals, radio call signs, and the like. After a time, he dismissed him to get some sleep before they landed.

As Duncan was leaving, Cade spoke up once more.

"Let's keep your ability between the two of us for now. It's probably better that way. No sense in making the men uneasy, right?"

Duncan couldn't imagine how his own healing ability would make men who called the Heretic their leader uneasy, but he nodded nonetheless.

Cade smiled and then leaned back into his chair.

The darkness around him seemed to swallow him whole.

# CHAPTER 8

T HE EARLY HOUR AND THE hum of the aircraft engine finally lulled Cade into sleep.

The dream came quickly.

In reality, the events had played out in horrible slowness.

In the dream, they always flashed past like a strobe light, one scene after another in endless succession.

Flash . . .

*"Williams here. Go ahead, Dispatch."*

*"Urgent call from your wife, Cade. Says she needs you to call her on a landline."*

*"Will do, Dispatch. Thanks for the relay."*

*Cade replaced the mike and turned to Jackson. "She probably wants me to pick up some milk and bread on the way home," he joked with his partner, Jackson, as he reached for his phone..*

*He dialed. Got a busy signal.*

*He hung up and tried again.*

*Still nothing.*

*He frowned, a small tendril of unease unfurling itself in his gut. He turned to Jackson. "I know I'm supposed to drop you off first, but would you mind if we go straight to my place? I can't get Gabbi on the phone."*

*"It will cost you a beer or two," Jackson said good-naturedly, and they had a deal.*

*Flash . . .*

*The interior lights were all out.*

*A tentacle of unease began to twist and turn in his gut, churning with a life of its own.*

*Something was wrong . . .*

*He parked in the driveway behind his wife's Audi.*

*The two of them got out of the car, Cade turning to say something to his partner.*

*Whatever it was, the words never left Cade's mouth.*

*Jackson suddenly buckled, just as a sharp report reached Cade's ears. A single flash of light came from the living room window off to his right and Cade knew Jackson had been taken down by gunfire.*

*"Run, Cade!" Gabrielle shouted from the darkened house.*

*Cade drew his gun and crouched behind his open car door, looking across the front seat to where Jackson lay slumped against the door, half-in and half-out of the vehicle.*

*"How bad?" he asked him.*

*"It hurts, but it's a clean through and through. He didn't hit anything vital." Jackson grunted in pain, then, "I'll call for backup."*

*But Cade was no longer listening. He leapt to his feet and rushed the front door, hoping his severe departure from standard police procedure would catch their assailant off guard long enough for him to make the safety of the porch.*

*Flash . . .*

*Inside.*

*A harsh laugh coming from the kitchen, down the hall in front of him.*

*The light from that room spilled out into the hallway, and movement in the shadows cast on the floor let Cade know there were at least two people in there. As he got closer, he could hear his wife sobbing.*

*With his gun held out before him in a shooter's stance, he took a deep breath and entered the room, a look of confidence on his face and fear in his heart.*

Flash . . .

*Cade knew the man standing in his kitchen with a pistol at his wife's head. Not personally, but he knew him nonetheless. He'd just spent the last five hours staring at his likeness in a police sketch, for he was wanted in connection with several recent homicides.*

*What Cade didn't understand was what the hell the Dorchester Slasher was doing in his home, threatening his wife.*

*Cade's arms moved slightly, and his aim settled on the center of the intruder's forehead.*

Flash . . .

*"What do you want?" Cade asked calmly.*

*"What do I want?" the intruder cackled.*

*The hairs on the back of Cade's arms stood at attention.*

*Cade's gun never wavered.*

*"Look. I can get you whatever you want," he said, indicating the radio on his belt. "All you've got to do is tell me what it is and let the woman go. We can work this out."*

*"Aren't you even curious, Officer Cade?"*

*"I'm sorry?"*

*"Aren't you curious? About why I'm in your house? Why I*

*shot your partner and am holding your wife hostage?" He giggled. " Aren't you curious about why I'm going to kill you both?"*

*Gabbi's eyes widened.*

*Flash . . .*

*Cade pulled the trigger and put a bullet through the right side of the Slasher's forehead.*

*The shot twisted his body back and away from Gabbi, as his finger tightened on the trigger.*

*The gun went off.*

*Flash . . .*

*Gabbi gasping, her eyes wide with shock. Cade walked over and put his arms around her, holding her tight. From out in the hall he could hear Jackson calling his name.*

*"We're in here. We're okay," Cade called back.*

*Flash...*

*One minute the Slasher was lying on his back, the next he was standing beside them. Before any of them could react, he grabbed Gabbi with one hand on either side of her head. Wrenching her away from Cade, he shoved his face against hers.*

*An inky blackness swelled forth from the corpse's mouth, enveloping Gabbi's face. Cade could hear her screaming, and beneath that a wet lapping sound, like a dog drinking from a bowl of water. He forced himself into motion, intent on getting that horrible thing away from his wife, and though he knew he was moving with his usual agility, each second seemed to pass with excruciating slowness. Out of the corner of his eye he could see Jackson's hand reaching for his weapon, taking what seemed like hours to move only a few inches.*

*Flash . . .*

*The thing released his wife, casting her away from itself*

across the room, her face a mess of raw flesh and blood, the outer layer of skin torn off. As she fell Cade could see her eyes were fixed and staring, and he knew in that second that he had lost her. His hand reached for his weapon as the corpse in front of him began shaking violently.

A crack suddenly appeared in the thing's forehead, starting at the bullet wound and flowing like rainwater down across its face. As Cade dragged his weapon free of its holster, the corpse's hands moved with dizzying speed and shoved its fingers into either side of the crack on its face.

Pulling sharply in either direction, it split its own skull in two, revealing the thing that lingered beneath.

For just a moment a face could be seen, with eyes a deep crimson and teeth gleaming blood red in the room's light. A malevolent smile crossed its face as it pulled the corpse's flesh down and away from its own form. A hint of wings could be seen as it sought to drag itself free from the fleshly remains in which it had been hiding.

Cade's hand came up, the pistol in it centering once more on its target. Peripherally, he could see Jackson's weapon doing the same.

Cade never had a chance to pull the trigger.

With the flick of its hands, the thing was free; the rest of the bodily remains flung away in either direction. One long clawed hang swung around and locked on Cade's, trapping his gun in its iron grip. The other slapped itself against the side of his face.

An inky black cloud of darkness flowed out of its hands and onto Cade's skin, burning his flesh with the intensity of molten steel.

In the back of his mind Cade could dimly hear himself screaming in agony and could feel the flesh on his face and hand *melting away.*

*In front of him, those eyes glowed with intelligence and an awful, inhuman glee . . .*

Flash . . .

Cade awoke.

He sat upright, the sound of his heart pounding in his chest. It sounded loud enough to him to be heard by his men in the forward compartment. He could feel the sweat running down his neck and pooling in the middle of his back beneath his shirt.

As he tried to center his thoughts, something moved in the darkness of the compartment.

He reacted the second he sensed the intrusion, moving out of the chair and into a crouch before it, balanced on the balls of his feet.

"Cade."

Just a word.

One simple word, spoken in a voice no louder than a whisper.

But a word that had all the power in the world when spoken by the woman he had loved more than life itself.

"Gabbi?" he asked, in a hoarse whisper.

When the figure did not respond, Cade reached beneath the shade of the lamp on the table next to him and turned on the switch.

In the sudden light, Cade discovered that he was alone.

The figure, if it had ever been there, was gone.

# CHAPTER 9

LOGAN CLIMBED THE CELLAR STAIRS, the howl of the revenant below causing a smile to dance upon his lips. They'd taken several of the Templars captive, on the off chance that they might be able to reveal something of importance. When they'd refused to answer his questions, he'd had them all slaughtered, then resurrected one at a time as revenants.

His questions were posed again.

Unfortunately, they'd been telling the truth. None of them had known anything of value.

Snatching them hadn't been completely in vain, however, as they were providing some merriment for Logan's acolytes, an experience that would only bond them even more securely to him as their leader.

As he moved through the house, headed for his nightly audience with the Other, he considered where the plan had taken them so far. The sheer audacity of it all was exhilarating. To steal one of the most powerful artifacts of Christianity right out from under the noses of those who had been tasked to guard it throughout the ages was a thrilling accomplishment. To do it with the help of one of their own was even more exquisite.

His smile grew wider at the thought.

Leaving the house, he crossed the grounds swiftly, a dark shadow against a darker background, with just the light of the moon to guide his way. Behind him only a slight disturbance in the dew-wet grass marked his passage.

Seconds later that, too, faded from view.

As he neared the old chapel, his pace slowed noticeably. The door stood slightly open to the night air, as he had known it would, just as it was every time he came here.

An unspoken invitation

The chapel had once been holy ground, but that was years ago. Any vestige of God that might have once inhabited the place had long since fled. Countless ceremonies and blood sacrifices had seen to that.

The Necromancer stepped through the door and moved down the center aisle to the edge of the raised altar platform, continuing around the side to its end.

*He waited in silence a moment, until a form moved out of the deeper darkness at the rear of the chapel behind the altar, back where the sacristy had once been. It did not come fully into the light; indeed, had never done so in the months since it had first unexpectedly taken up residence here. Once, the Necromancer had gotten a brief glimpse of the creature, a quick vision of a humanoid form, but that had been all he'd seen before it had retreated into the darkness it seemed to prefer. He hoped never to repeat the experience. Summoning his courage, Logan began.*

*"The search for the Spear continues, though we have recently begun to narrow the area of interest. The one they call the Heretic has been assigned to the case, just as you predicted, and*

*is even now following the trail we have laid out for him."*

"Good." The voice was deep, guttural, and it danced along his nerve endings like grease on a spit, grease that pops and cracks with searing heat as it drips into the fire. "You have done as I have asked, then?"

The Necromancer nodded, knowing from past experience that the other could see him quite clearly despite the cloying darkness of the chapel's interior.

A sound came from it then, a sound that might have been a laugh though not one that could ever have been produced by human vocal cords. When it had exhausted its good humor, it went on. "Set out the bait. It is time we caught our prey."

"As you wish."

The Necromancer bowed curtly and backed out of the chamber, never taking his gaze away from the thing that stood before him.

Despite their temporary partnership, the Necromancer had no delusions about the nature of his ally.

It would destroy him on a whim, just as it had decided to aid him.

He had come too far, was too close to his goal, to allow that to happen. He would give it no reason to doubt him.

Not until he was ready.

# CHAPTER 10

T HE FOUR MEMBERS OF ECHO'S command team arrived
at the Cincinnati International Airport around 6 A.M.
local time. A rented Ford Explorer was waiting for
them in the private hangar where the pilot parked the aircraft.
Their destination was about an hour's drive north, and after
transferring their gear into the vehicle the team wasted no time
getting under way. Cade and Olsen climbed in back, with Riley
behind the wheel and Duncan riding shotgun.

Cade stared out the rear passenger window. He couldn't get
the echo of Gabbi's voice out of his head, calling out his name
the night before.

But Gabbi was dead and, as far as he knew, at rest. In the five
years since her passing he'd never once encountered her in the
Beyond, never had even a single hint that her spirit still
languished there. He'd long ago come to the conclusion that she
had passed on to whatever version of an afterlife someone of her
sweet grace deserved. And yet . . .

*And yet you hope it was her, don't you? You hope it was*
*because you miss her and because every single day living*

*without her seems to be a waste. No matter what it would mean to her, to be trapped in that half state of existence like the phantoms you encounter in the Beyond, you still want to believe, don't you?*

Grudgingly, Cade had to admit to himself that it was true. Every morning when he awoke to find himself without her was another day in which his heart broke anew.

*Cade's own views of heaven and hell had been drastically altered when he first looked into the Beyond. It would have been impossible for them not to have changed. Raised as a Catholic, he'd believed in an afterlife based on one's faith in the Savior and had scoffed at notions of ghosts and goblins as far back as he could remember.*

His encounter with the Adversary had changed all that.

If he had not discovered the Order when he had, he probably wouldn't have survived. His pain, confusion, and fear would have driven him over the edge. The Templars had helped him resurrect a framework around his beliefs; allowed him to hang on to the cherished notion that his wife's soul had moved on to a better place. Those aware of the existence of the Beyond suggested it served as a sort of Purgatory, pointed out that a woman as faithful and true as his wife would never choose to stay in such a place. Gradually, they taught him that Man was not alone in the world, that there were beings of darkness and destruction that walked among Man every day. At least in part, the Order had convinced him that some of his older notions of faith and justice still held sway, that the Templars were the earthly equivalent of a group of guardian angels, appointed by the Church to protect Man from creatures such as the Adversary.

And so he had joined them.

*But what if it was Gabbi?* Cade asked himself. *What then?*

*What did that mean for your cherished beliefs? What if she really was out there? What if she had been there all this time and you hadn't noticed, wrapped up as you are in your hunger for vengeance?*

Cade couldn't allow himself to contemplate an answer. If it weren't for his desire for revenge, he probably would have followed Gabbi and ended his life long before this. It would have been simpler that way.

*But a vow is a vow and you've still got to fulfill yours. While the Adversary lives, the hunt is still on,* the voice in the back of his head whispered.

*The hunt is still on.*

Putting the question of Gabbi's appearance on the back burner for the time being, Cade turned his attention back to the issue at hand.

"All right, Olsen. Take us through it."

As Nick pulled out his PDA and called up the information, Cade noted approvingly that Duncan gave his teammate his undivided attention. Cade knew without a doubt that Riley was listening as well, despite the fact that the big man didn't take his attention off the road.

"Okay. Initial reports show we've got a similar situation to the one we just left in Connecticut – an attack late at night, signs of a heavy firefight, no survivors." Nick began. "Two major differences from Ravensgate. This time, the small cemetery on the grounds was disturbed. Most of the graves were torn up and the contents strewn about. Whatever they were looking for, they were certainly thorough"

"Witnesses?"

Olsen shook his head. "No. And that brings us to the other issue. When the general alert went out last night, each of the commanderies was required to report back to the Preceptor. Templeton did not respond, and so a team was sent out to investigate. They found the place abandoned."

"What do you mean, abandoned?" asked Duncan.

Olsen turned to face him. "While we're assuming the commandery staff are dead, we're not entirely positive. Despite the signs of a major confrontation, there wasn't a single body left at the scene."

Riley spoke up from the front seat. "There were eighty-eight men stationed at Templeton."

Olsen caught his eye in the rearview mirror.

"Yes. There were," he replied, with the emphasis on *were*.

\* \* \*

They were met at the gate by several soldiers from the commandery in Folkenberg, some seventy-five miles to the north. It was the same unit that had been sent to investigate after Templeton's personnel failed to report in following the alert the night before.

Cade interviewed them at some length, but they didn't know anything more than they'd already reported; when they arrived, they'd discovered evidence of a firefight but found the commandery empty, abandoned.

Leaving the Folkenberg troops stationed at the gates, Echo Team made its own swift search of the manor house, confirming what they had been told. The evening meal lay cold in the communal dining hall, half-eaten. The armory had been opened, its weapons distributed. Bullet casings and bloodstains littered the floor behind makeshift barricades.

But there were no bodies.

No survivors.

They spent two hours in the house, then turned their attention to the cemetery.

It had been ransacked.

Desecrated.

Graves had been dug open, the dirt stark against the lush green grass. The unearthed coffins had been ripped apart, their contents spilled across the lawn. A rib cage was jammed between the branches of a newly planted rosebush. An age-yellowed skull with its lower jaw missing and one eye socket stuffed with mud lay in the middle of a pedestrian walkway.

This was the intentional destruction of hallowed ground, a vile disturbance of sanctified remains that appeared to have no legitimate purpose behind it. Anger stirred in Cade's gut at the sight.

A quick examination showed that while most of the graves had been torn up haphazardly, one of them had been carefully excavated. He decided to start there.

Duncan stood next to that open grave, ready to assist him if he needed it. Riley and Olsen were several yards away, but facing in the other direction, guarding the approaches in anticipation of trouble. Things weren't right there, and Cade had no intention of being caught unawares.

He removed his gloves and placed them in his pocket before kneeling in the earth next to the open grave. The smell of freshly turned earth, moldering death, and stale air met his nostrils; but he barely noticed the stench as he mentally prepared himself to do what must be done.

The parapsychologists and those who studied psychic phenomena had a formal name for what he did. Psychometry, they called it, the ability to divine facts about an object or its owner through physical contact.

Cade had an easier name for it.

He simply called it his Gift.

It had been seven years since the Gift was thrust upon him, but in that time he still had not grown comfortable using it. He wondered if he ever would.

It wasn't the loss of tactile sensation that bothered him so much. He'd become accustomed to how things felt through the thin material of his gloves. And it wasn't as if he was unable to touch things at all. When he was at home safely surrounded by his own possessions, he would often move about the house without his gloves on, doing just that for hours at a time. Remembering what it felt like to run his fingers over cut stone. Feeling the velvety touch of flour as it sifted between his fingers. Holding a book in his hands and testing the quality of the paper between his thumb and forefinger. His home was his sanctuary; no one else was allowed inside, in order to limit the psychic latencies that might be left behind.

Only the intimate touch of another human being was unavailable; that level of sustained contact would bring with it such an overwhelming rush of emotional residue that he would be hard-pressed to understand where he ended and his partner began. Had Gabbi lived, things might have been different, but, in the aftermath of her death, Cade had ceased to care about human contact, at least in that fashion, and so this troubled him far less than others might expect.

It was possible that his discomfort with his Gift grew from the fact that using it brought a degree of physical danger, though he was never one to shy away from the possibility of physical injury. On past occasions he had emerged from a session confused, disoriented, at times even uncertain of his own identity. Once, during a particularly violent viewing, he regained consciousness with knife slashes across his chest.

He suspected the true reason for his discomfort lay in the way the Gift had come to him. There was little doubt that the Adversary meant to kill him on that summer night and had only failed by the smallest of margins. But something had been left behind, some kind of residue or catalyst that resulted in his Gift, his Sight.

He glanced around, making certain his men were in their proper places. Riley, standing off to his right, returned his look with a somber nod. Olsen, stationed behind him, smiled ruefully, as if to say, "Don't worry, boss, I've got your back." Cade had no doubt that he did. It was the newcomer he questioned; how he reacted about what Cade was going to do would say a lot about his future with the unit. He checked to be certain that Duncan was where he should be, on the opposite side of the grave, out of immediate reach if he objected to what Cade was doing but close enough to help if things got hairy.

The top had been split into several sections though the bottom remained intact. A large section of the lid rested in front of Cade, its silk lining torn and stained from contact with the mud and debris around it.

Reaching out, Cade placed his right hand palm down against the outer surface of a torn and discarded portion of the coffin lid.

*Darkness.*

*A light breeze rustling the edges of his cowl.*

*The steady motion of the shovel as it went up and down.*

*He was falling behind, and that would never do. He could be punished for that. He needed to hurry up!*

*Anticipation.*

*Excitement.*

*A glimpse of several robed and hooded men, staring down into the hole as he worked to complete his task.*

*Would the Council get its answer tonight or would it need to raise another one?*

*He hoped it was the latter; he liked playing God.*

The images and rush of the other's feelings came and went, there and gone again before Cade could focus on them. In mere seconds they had faded from view.

Cade removed his hand and shook his head to clear it.

"You all right, boss?" Riley asked, his deep voice breaking the silence that had settled over the group.

"Fine," Cade replied, without looking up. He tested several other places near where he had touched the lid the first time, but any remaining impressions proved elusive.

With Duncan looking on curiously, Cade pushed aside the remains of the lid and turned his attention to the casket. The interior lining was stained with mold and other substances that Cade was in no real hurry to identify. The silk itself was faded and dull, evidence that the interment was not a recent one. He found a clear spot large enough to accommodate his hand and reached out to touch the lining.

*Darkness.*

*Peace.*

*Serenity.*

*Pain.*

*A harsh, savage pain that ripped through his body with all the grace of a hot spear.*

*A voice was calling him, demanding his return, and he was too weak to stop himself from obeying.*

*The pain increased, the voice grew louder, until he could barely hear his own screams . . .*

Cade yanked his hand away, ending the sensation, and looked up into the face of his new recruit, now kneeling close by, a concerned look on his face.

"Are you okay?" Duncan asked, though he made no move to touch the Echo Team leader.

Cade nodded.

"Just what, exactly, are you doing?" Duncan asked.

"He's looking into the past," Riley replied for him, as he watched his commander closely to be certain he wasn't needed.

Duncan looked over at the other man. "The past?"

Riley nodded, turning his attention back to their surroundings now that he was satisfied that Cade was all right. "It's one of the reasons those idiots call him the Heretic. He receives visions through his touch."

"Is that true?" Duncan asked Cade.

In control once more, Cade replied, "It's a simplification of what really happens, but, yes, it's true. A more accurate description might be that I experience the final thoughts and emotions of the last person to come in contact with the object I'm handling, but Riley's explanation works just as well. Except that he forgot to tell you I have no control over it, that it happens whenever I touch anything, whether I want it to or not.

"I'm going to try again, try to get a clearer picture of what I'm seeing. Something's not right. If you see something unusual, if I start to shake, bleed, or otherwise look like I'm in danger, I want you to grab me by my shirt and pull me away from the casket. Understand?"

"Yes," Duncan replied, even though it was obvious to Cade that he really didn't.

*Welcome to the big leagues, kid.*

Taking a deep breath, Cade placed his hand on the remains of the coffin for a third time.

*A searing hunger coursed through him as he climbed to his feet, a hunger so strong it felt like pain.*

*Ahead of him, he could see the dark-cloaked forms of several people gathered in a circle around another, taller figure. The one in the center was calling his name, demanding he come forth, demanding he respond to the summons.*

*He was filled with a strong compulsion to obey, but he did his best to ignore the voice. The smell of human flesh so close it made him dizzy with hunger, and all he wanted to do was feed. When he tried to move forward, however, he tripped over something in his path and fell heavily to the ground. Pulling himself back up, his gaze fell to the object on the ground.*

*It was a young woman, bound and gagged, left lying in the dirt at his feet. Her eyes gaped wide, and she was trying to scream, but the gag muffled the sound and caused her to choke on her own fear.*

*The scent of her sweet skin was strong and filled his nostrils, the fear rich and ripe.*

*He pounced, all other thoughts forgotten.*

*His teeth ripped into her tender flesh, and her hot blood flowed.*

*The struggles and muffled screams eventually stopped.*

*The voice soon returned, asking questions.*

*This time, his hunger satisfied for the moment, he didn't mind answering.*

With a jolt Cade came out of the trance only to find himself being held to the ground by Riley, the big man's arm around his neck. The sharp taste of blood was strong in his mouth, and he could feel its wetness flowing down his chin.

On the ground a few feet away sat Duncan, his left arm

cradling his right, blood flowing from a small wound on his forearm. Nick was kneeling beside him, trying to stop the flow of blood.

"He bit me," Duncan said, incredulous.

Cade didn't hear him. He pulled himself free of Riley's hold and sat up, moving to face the other man. He now understood what they were facing and the knowledge filled him with fear.

"Revenants," he said. "They're raising revenants."

As the others watched, horrified at what they had just seen and heard, Cade calmly turned and spit Duncan's blood from his mouth.

# CHAPTER 11

R EVENANTS.

Corpses reanimated through the use of dark magick, souls forced back into decomposing flesh and infused with a taste for living flesh. Abominations against the Lord.

After Cade's revelation, the fact that the commandery was empty took on a deeper, more ominous meaning. The dead weren't just missing, and Echo Team had to contend with the very real possibility that the bodies of their brethren had gotten up again under their own power. Being brought back in such a fashion would be terrible for anyone; it would be a particularly hellish experience for the devout Knights who had given their lives for the cause.

Duncan's mind reeled.

Considering what they knew, none of them felt comfortable remaining at the site of the attack. The decision was made to spend the evening at the Folkenberg commandery, roughly an hour's drive to the west.

Back in the truck, with Riley once more behind the wheel,

Olsen did his best to bind Duncan's wound while Cade got on the phone to let the others know they were on their way.

Turning to Olsen, Duncan asked, "Does this kind of thing happen a lot?"

"No, you're the first subordinate he's bitten."

Duncan wasn't amused. "That's not what . . ."

Nick chuckled. "Relax, kid. I'm just trying to lighten the mood. Like I said before, the commander's methods can sometimes be a little unorthodox, but he gets the job done. At least now we know what we're up against."

The sergeant pulled the bandage tight and the sharp stab of pain that accompanied the move caused Duncan's retort to die stillborn in his throat.

* * *

Their destination, a small commandery under the control of Knight Captain Noel Stanton, was situated in a heavily wooded and sparsely populated area of Folkenberg. Like many of the commanderies Cade had visited across the United States, this one had been established on the grounds of a large estate. It was separated from the surrounding properties by a large stone wall that encircled it.

The entrance lane ran parallel to that wall for some time before they came to the gate, giving Cade plenty of opportunity to scope out the cameras and security devices concealed along its length.

They were met at the gate by an armed guard wearing the insignia of a local security company, who questioned them about who they were there to see, then returned to his guard shack, apparently to ring the main desk to be certain they had an appointment.

Satisfied with the answer he received over the phone, he opened the gates and waved them through without leaving his shack a second time.

If it hadn't been for the signet ring bearing the Templar cross on the guard's right hand, Duncan never would have known he was a member of the Order. Hiding in plain sight was one of the Order's greatest assets, and Duncan knew that the ruse would certainly fool the average passerby.

Riley drove through the open gates and down the road leading into the estate proper. The commandery was an older brick mansion with a slate roof and white columns dominating its front entrance. A young initiate was standing on the steps awaiting their arrival when they pulled to a stop at the foot of the steps.

"Knight Commander Williams?" the novice asked, as the team exited the vehicle and approached.

Cade nodded.

"I'm Novitiate Parkins. Captain Stanton asked me to take you to his study immediately upon arrival."

"Very good."

The team was escorted into a large room tastefully decorated in dark woods and fabrics. A heavy oak desk sat before a large bay window that looked out on marble statuary standing in the center of the well-lit grounds. An area rug surrounded by several armchairs was arranged in front of the fireplace on the opposite side of the room.

A short, stocky man in his midforties, with dark hair cut in a military fashion, stood behind the desk and came forward immediately as the other men entered the room, introducing himself as Knight Captain Stanton. He shook each man's hand, only hesitating briefly when he came to Cade.

*So my reputation precedes me,* Cade thought, as he noted the other man's discomfort.

"Please, have a seat," said the captain, indicating the chairs.

"Thank you, Captain, but that's not necessary. We've been on alert for the last several days now and really just want to grab the chance to get some rest. A few spare rooms and access to the network is all that we require."

The captain nodded. "Of course, Commander. I'll have Parkins here get you situated. If there is anything else you need, please don't hesitate to ask."

Cade shook the captain's hand once more and followed Parkins out of the office, his men at his heels.

Back out in the hallway, Cade dismissed the others just as the bells rang for Compline. Despite being tired, Riley, Olsen, and Duncan joined several of the locals for the evening Mass, all of them feeling the need to reconnect with their faith and purpose in light of what they had seen and heard that day. The sermon was about duty and honor in times of strife, appropriate for the circumstances, and Duncan felt the weight on his soul lift slightly as he settled into the familiar rhythms of the Latin responses. Several times during the service he turned his head to look back into the crowd gathered in the sanctuary, trying to locate Cade, but the commander was nowhere to be found.

After the ceremony, he raised the issue with Riley as they moved off down the hallway toward their assigned quarters.

"No, you didn't miss him. He wasn't there," Riley replied.

"Oh." Duncan wasn't sure what to make of that, but what Riley said next was even more troubling.

"The Commander hasn't attended Mass in quite some time."

Duncan reached out and grasped the other man by the elbow,

stopping him. "He doesn't attend Mass? Why not?" A senior Templar officer not attending regular service was highly unusual.

Riley gazed at him silently for a moment, weighing his answer, then pulled free with a jerk of his arm. "He just doesn't. Leave it at that," Riley said over his shoulder, as he stepped away.

Duncan should have expected it, but the realization that most of the rumors about his new commanding officer might just be true left him almost breathless. He slumped against the nearest wall, his thoughts in turmoil. He'd only been with the unit a few days, and already he'd been forced to deal with sorcerers, revenants, and a commanding officer who'd seemingly turned his back on the Lord. It was almost too much to take.

Still, he had little choice. The Preceptor had agreed to his reassignment for a reason and he'd do his best to live up to his superior's expectations.

Yet as he walked off to his quarters, he was unable to banish either his sense of growing sense of discomfort or the feeling of Cade's teeth clamped tight on the fleshy part of his arm.

* * *

Later that night, Riley shook Cade awake.

"We've got trouble," he said, his expression grim.

Cade nodded and ordered him to assemble the rest of Echo Team's sergeants in a conference room for an immediate meeting.

When he arrived, Cade joined them at the table, and said simply, "Talk to me."

As usual, Olsen did the briefing. "About thirty minutes ago

we received a call from Father Joseph Burns, pastor of St. Margaret's in Broward Township. Burns is one of our local contacts. He was working late in his office at the rear of the church when a noise out front caught his attention. Concerned about vandalism, he wandered into the sanctuary to find someone standing before the altar and staring in fascination at the cross above it.

"Father Burns called out to the intruder, asking him what he wanted. At the sound of the priest's voice, the figure spun around and charged. At which point the good father got the fright of his life. The priest kept his wits about him and managed to outmaneuver the intruder, trapping him in the sacristy to the right of the altar. He took these with his digital camera," said Olsen, passing a folder across the table to Cade.

Inside were a series of photographs, obviously printed out on a home computer. Even so, they told the tale quite eloquently.

Shot through a small window in the door leading to the sacristy, the photos were of a man who'd obviously been dead for several months. His hair had fallen out in clumps, exposing skin covered with a thin patina of mold. One eye stared at the camera; the other was nothing more than a gaping socket. He was pounding on the other side of the window glass with what was left of his right hand, the bones of the fourth and fifth fingers clearly visible. Small bits of flesh were left on the glass after every blow.

"We've had a few other scattered reports intercepted through the police bands. Mysterious shapes glimpsed roaming through the woods, children being frightened by a stranger looking in through the windows, that sort of thing. I'm willing to bet they were all caused by the same individual."

After glancing at the photos, Cade passed them to the rest of his assembled men, letting them each take a good, long look. He stared off into space for several long moments while they did so, lost in thought, then said, "Okay. Here's what we're going to do."

\* \* \*

Cade emerged from the manor house twenty minutes later to find a Blackhawk helicopter warming up on the front lawn. The vehicle's exterior was painted in dark colors and had neither identification nor insignia. Riley stood by the open door, his superior's Kevlar vest and communications rig in one hand.

Crossing the lawn, Cade ducked under the rotating blades and took the items from his sergeant. He slipped into the vest, pulled the straps tight, then climbed aboard, finding a seat next to Olsen. Riley wasted no time in following him inside. He flashed a hand signal to the pilot, and the chopper lifted off into the darkness of the evening sky before the sergeant had finished settling into a seat on the other side of the aircraft next to Duncan. Cade pulled on the communications rig and jacked into the panel above his head. Keying the mike, he asked, "How are we doing?"

Olsen had his laptop open, his fingers dancing across the keyboard as he monitored external traffic through the communications net, and didn't look up from the screen as he replied. "We're good. I've touched base with Father Burns. His guest is still locked up tight in the sacristy."

Cade nodded his understanding and turned to look out the still-open door. The Blackhawk was moving quickly through the night, following the Ohio River as it made its way north. Clouds could be seen on the horizon, but for the moment the weather was fine, and visibility was good. At their current rate of speed, he estimated it would be about a ten minute journey to Broward Township.

They passed the short trip in silence. Like Cade, most of the men were thinking about a resurrected Knight trapped like a rat in a small room, his body literally falling apart around him. It was not a comforting image.

Leaving the river behind, the pilot cut across country at treetop level. It was only a moment or two before the white spire of a church steeple could be seen in the distance. The church was set at the edge of town on a large stretch of property surrounded by a thick grove of elms. It was far enough away from the rest of the community that they ran little risk of being seen, so Cade had the pilot set down momentarily on the back lawn. Cade and his men quickly disembarked, and the pilot took the chopper back up again to wait high overhead for their signal.

As the four Knights approached, the rear door of the rectory opened, silhouetting the man standing there, waiting for them.

"Father Burns?" Cade asked, extending his hand. "Commander Williams."

"Thank God you've arrived, Commander. This way please." The priest looked askance at the weapons the men carried, but he made no comment about their presence as he led them through the rectory and into the church proper.

"It's been quiet in there for the last fifteen minutes," Burns said, indicating the door of the sacristy with his hand.

Cade stepped up and peered inside.

The room was small; a set of floor-to-ceiling cabinets stood opposite a waist-high counter containing a sink, with wooden cupboard bolted to the wall above it.

Against the far wall crouched the revenant. It was holding a purple stole, obviously taken from the pile of vestments that littered the floor in front of the open cabinets. Intent on its prize, the creature didn't appear to notice him.

Cade stepped away from the window and looked at the others. "Okay. I want standard entry procedure. Olsen, you've got the door. Riley, you're with me. Duncan, I want you on overwatch. If it gets by us, it will be up to you to stop it."

Cade removed his gun and handed it to Father Burns. "Hold this for me, will ya?"

The elderly priest accepted it uneasily. "Aren't you going to need this?" he asked.

"No," Cade replied, as he pulled two flash bangs off his belt. "We need to take this thing alive, if you can call it that." He turned to Riley. "When Olsen opens the door, I'll toss the flash bangs. I want you to follow with two more. Hopefully, they'll be enough to bring the thing down. As soon as they go off, we rush in and secure it."

Commonly used by law enforcement groups worldwide, the flash bangs were designed to emit a blinding light while at the same time punishing the eardrums with a loud crack. Cade had always pictured it as being caught between a thunderclap and a lightning bolt. The assault on the senses was enough to send most suspects to their knees, their senses reeling. He hoped it would have the same effect on the revenant.

"If we get in there and things go to shit, don't hesitate to take it down."

"Roger that," said Riley.

"We ready?"

The other three men nodded.

"All right then, let's do it."

As the priest moved deeper into the nave so that he was well out of the way, the other four men got into position. Cade and Riley on the right-hand side of the door, Olsen in front of it, key in hand. Duncan stood several feet back, his gun pointed directly ahead in case the creature somehow got past the others.

Cade counted it down on his fingers – one, two, three. On four, Olsen slid the key smoothly into the lock, gave it a sharp twist, and pulled the door partially open, giving the others time to toss their flash bangs into the room, before slamming it shut once more.

This was the dangerous moment, with the door unlocked and all of them looking away so that the pulsing light of the devices wouldn't blind them, too. If the revenant chose that moment to charge the door . . .

But it did not.

The flash bangs went off, then Cade and Riley were rushing inside, Olsen at their heels.

A few moments later they stepped back out of the sacristy carrying the revenant between them, its hands and feet secured with Zip-ties and the purple stole it had been holding doubling as a gag. Cade received his weapon from the grateful Father Burns, while Riley called the chopper in for the extraction.

The priest watched from the rectory door once more as the Templars crossed the lawn, tossed their captive into the back of the helicopter, and lifted off without a backward glance.

* * *

Once back at the commandery, Cade left Olsen in charge of the prisoner's relocation. He needed some time alone to try and marshal his thoughts; things were happening quickly and he hadn't had nearly enough time to consider the implications.

After informing the captain of the guard where he would be, he set off on a long walk around the commandery grounds.

He puzzled over the information his team had uncovered so far. There were gaping holes in it, but he thought he was beginning to see a form to it, a sense of pattern appearing out of the chaos.

He had yet to determine how the Enemy was learning the locations of the commanderies, however, and that set him to thinking about the idea that there was a mole in the Order. Despite the Preceptor's suspicions, he had yet to see anything that might confirm that idea. There was more than one way to uncover the Order's existence.

Which brought him to the issue of the revenants. Obviously, the former Templars would know the location of the Order's hideaways. It was reasonable to think that the Enemy was resurrecting the dead in order to question them, to learn as much about the Order and its various sites as possible. That also might explain some of the haphazardness to the individual attacks. Obviously crisscrossing the Atlantic region wasn't the most effective way to assault the Order, but if they were forced to attack only the sites revealed to them in this fashion, they'd have little choice in the selection process.

Yet that didn't seem right to Cade. It was cumbersome, for one. And it certainly didn't guarantee success. From what he'd seen so far, their enemy had been well organized and pulled of its operations with skill and expertise. A foe like that wouldn't rely on the random chance that it might learn something from a half-crazed revenant.

Full circle again; back to the mole. Cade couldn't ignore the fact that somehow the Enemy had learned about Ravensgate. Enough that it had been able to penetrate the defenses and slaughter every soldier stationed there, without leaving behind a single witness or physical clue for anyone to work with.

That implied inside knowledge, as the Preceptor had suggested.

Frustrated and knowing his lack of understanding about the Enemy's objective was probably coloring his ability to make sense of the details in front of him, Cade decided it was time to see if they could learn anything from the man they'd captured in Broward.

Turning toward the manor house, he headed back in that direction with a determined stride and a fresh sense of expectation.

# CHAPTER 12

T HE REST OF HIS COMMAND squad was standing around the table in the observation area of Interrogation Room Four when Cade arrived.

Duncan moved to confront him the moment he entered the room. "This is ridiculous," he said, gesturing over his shoulder to the prisoner they had secured in the next room. "That *thing* needs to be destroyed. Immediately."

"That thing, as you so quaintly put it, is a former member of this Order." Cade replied sternly. "You will treat him with the respect he deserves, no matter what his present condition. Is that clear?"

But rather than getting him to acquiesce, the reminder that the thing in the next room had once been one of their own only inflamed the young Templar further. "Treat him with respect? You've got to be kidding me! The only way to do that is to put a bullet through his skull and let him rest. This," - he indicated the revenant seated in the next room - "this is simply obscene."

It had been a long, difficult day, and Cade had had enough. He stepped close, crowding the other man with his bulk, and this time his voice had a steel edge to its tone. "Your opinion has been noted. Now shut up. My duty is to find the threat to our Order and put a stop to it. I intend to do that. Right now, that man in there is our best hope of doing so, and I'm going to use him as much as I have to in order to accomplish that goal. If you don't like it, you can remove yourself from the room. Is that clear?"

They stared each other down for several tense seconds before the younger man looked away, nodded, and stepped aside.

Cade crossed the room and looked through the one-way mirror into the interrogation room, where their guest was shackled to the wall. The chains were long enough to let him sit on the floor with his head between his knees, so Cade was unable to see his face.

But he didn't need to.

"You recognize him, don't you?" Cade asked, looking back over his shoulder at his second-in-command.

Riley grimaced but nodded his head. "George Winston. Bravo Team, wasn't he?"

"That's right. Assault squad, if I remember correctly." Cade turned to Olsen. "What's happened since they brought him in?"

"He fought against the restraints at first, pulling on the chains as if he might get them to pop free through brute force alone. Ended up slamming himself against the wall a couple of times too. When that didn't work he tried chewing through his arm, but gave that up when he tasted his own flesh. Since then he's just sat there, waiting, as if he knows we'll come to him eventually. He's been that way for over an hour now."

"Just what, exactly, do we hope to learn from this...thing?" Duncan asked.

"I don't know how much we can learn," Cade replied without

turning. "But right now he's the only clue we've got. If there's a possibility he can tell us anything, we have to try." He looked at Riley. "What do you think?"

"I wouldn't want to be trapped in that room if it gets loose, that's what I think."

"Agreed. Which is why I want you and Olsen on the other side of this doorway. If anything goes wrong, don't hesitate. Get inside and put it down, clear?"

Both men nodded.

Cade continued. "Duncan, get with Captain Stanton and find out if there is anyone here who served with Bravo Team during the last five years. If there is, I want him here ASAP. Having a priest nearby might not be a bad idea either, so see who you can scare up."

"Will do."

"Good. Let's move, people."

When Cade turned back to the mirror, he found Winston staring at it from the other side.

Despite the fact that the mirror was one-way, Cade was sure the revenant could see him.

To test his theory, Cade took three steps to his right.

Winston's head turned to track his movement.

Back to the left.

Again, the revenant watched him move.

It seemed to Cade that, in the revenant's eyes, there was a deep sense of longing.

But whether that longing was over what he had lost or simply the desire for his next meal, Cade couldn't tell.

It took fifteen minutes to get the details squared away.

Duncan returned with two men in tow. "Father Garcon, Corporal Reese, this is Knight Commander Williams." To Cade he said, "I've explained to them both what we need. Reese spent three years with Bravo before being transferred here last year."

Garcon, a heavyset, balding man, was clearly the priest. Which made the younger man dressed in technician's coveralls the former Bravo Team member. Cade led him over to the observation window and let him get a good long look at the former Knight on the other side, then said, "How well did you know him?"

Without taking his gaze away from the glass, Reese said, "We were on the same squad for about eighteen months, sir. Spent some of our downtime together on leave."

"So he would know you on sight?"

"Normally, I'd say yes, sir." He didn't have to explain his hesitation, given Winston's condition.

"Good enough. Despite his present condition, the Winston you knew still exists inside that shell. We need to reach him, get him to talk to us. I'm hoping that a familiar face might help him focus on who he was, rather than on what he has become, so I need you to go into that room with us when the times comes. Can you do that?"

Reese hesitated, swallowed hard, and nodded.

Cade clapped him on the shoulder. "Good man."

The commander walked back over to the priest. "Thank you for coming, Father. My sergeant explained the situation to you?"

The older man nodded, though he was clearly uncomfortable. He had studiously avoided glancing at the observation window since entering the room, and Cade noticed that Garcon's hands were trembling as he unpacked his portable Mass kit on the table before him.

"This man is a former Knight of the Order. His belief in God might still survive his present condition. Your presence there could be a great comfort to him."

Garcon finally looked up, meeting Cade's gaze, and the commander immediately knew he had been mistaken. What he had taken for fear was actually anger. "And you, Knight Commander? Shall I pray for you as well?" The priest, obviously, did not approve of his methods.

Cade ignored the question and the thinly veiled insubordination. "Just do your job, Father. I'll worry about my own soul, thanks."

Turning away from Garcon, Cade addressed the rest of the men in the room. "All right. Let's do this."

When Olsen and Riley were in their places, Cade stepped inside the interrogation room and moved quickly to one side of the door, as Reese and Father Garcon did the same on the other side. Once they were in, Cade quickly closed the door behind them.

Winston watched them enter the room without getting up. His gaze lingered on Reese for several moments, and a low moan escaped his mouth when he caught sight of the purple stole around the elderly priest's neck, but that was all. Neither man elicited more than a mild reaction.

The revenant turned to look at Cade.

He stared at him for a long moment, unmoving.

Then he went berserk.

Winston surged to his feet, straining at his chains and gnashing his teeth as an eerie howling cry burst forth from his mouth.

Reese and Garcon recoiled, moving for the door; but Cade remained steady, knowing the chains would hold.

Two feet away from the commander, the chains pulled Winston up short with a suddenness that yanked him off his feet.

He slammed to the floor, only to thrash around wildly as he tried to pull himself closer to Cade.

Cade tried several times to get the revenant's attention, to ask him some questions, but to no avail. The creature was starving and it was clear to Cade that he wasn't going to get anything useful out of him until something was done about it.

Cade turned to face the one-way mirror, and said, "I need a knife. A sharp one. And a pressure bandage."

It took only a few moments before the door opened, and the two items he'd requested were slipped inside. Cade took it, withdrew the commando-style combat knife from its sheath, and tested the edge.

A fine line of blood welled up where he ran his thumb along the blade.

It would do.

The creature settled down at the sight of the blood and watched Cade closely, as if sensing his intent. Winston's hunger was like a phantom presence, palpable in its intensity.

Under the creature's watchful gaze Cade knelt and rolled up the cuff of his right pant leg. He set the knife's edge against the skin of his calf and drew it down sharply. A wafer-thin piece of flesh rolled up behind the blade and fell to the floor. Blood flowed, hot and sharp. Cade gritted his teeth against the pain and slapped the pressure bandage over the wound. Once he was certain the bandage would stop the bleeding, he bent over and carefully picked up his offering.

The creature watched him, his eyes wide and staring, his hunger a pulsing need that filled the room.

Cade cut the strip in half and tossed one section to Winston.

The revenant's hand shot out and snatched the offering out of midair. He shoved it in his mouth and chewed quickly.

With that, Reese had seen enough. He banged on the door and exited the room quickly when Olsen opened it up. Surprisingly, Father Garcon remained inside. Cade could hear him whispering a prayer of mercy for the unfortunate man before them and turned to see if it would have any effect.

Winston, however, didn't notice.

After feeding on even that small piece of flesh, an immediate change seemed to come over him. His gaze grew more alert, his attention more focused on the man standing before him.

Cade gave it another try.

"Listen to me, George. I know you can understand me if you try."

The revenant's gaze never left the remaining strip of human flesh Cade held in his other hand.

"I'm going to ask you some more questions. If you answer them, I'll give you this." Cade held up the flesh.

If the revenant could have salivated, Cade was certain he would have.

"Do you understand me, George?"

Slowly, Winston raised his gaze from the meat to look Cade in the eyes. With a barely noticeable twitch, he indicated his understanding.

"Good."

Cade paused, considering, and then asked, "Who did this to you, George? Do you know who it was?"

Winston tried to speak, but his reply sounded like nothing so much as a choking bark.

"I'm sorry, George, I didn't understand. Try again."

Again the sound.

It was obvious that he was trying to cooperate, but the damage to his vocal cords had progressed too far for him to be understood.

Cade was not yet ready to give up. It was clear that the revenant still possessed the intelligence he had held in life; the person that had once been George Winston was still locked inside that body, struggling to get out. If he could, he should be able to tell them what they wanted to know. But first Cade would have to figure out a way to allow that to happen.

As it turned out, it was the revenant himself who found the solution. With one hand he traced the number nine on the floor beside him.

"Nine?" Cade repeated aloud, puzzled by the answer.

The revenant repeated the gesture, his eyes locked on the strip of flesh Cade still held in his hand.

"There were nine of them?"

The revenant's head twitched, and his hands clenched into fists as he sought to maintain control. His hunger was growing. Calming himself, he nodded.

"Okay. The number nine." Cade didn't understand what Winston was referring to, so he moved on, hoping a different question might elicit a more understandable response.

"What did they want?"

Ignoring the question, the creature suddenly lunged at Cade, his hunger taking his self-control.

Cade didn't even flinch. He'd positioned himself carefully, and he simply watched as the revenant fetched up against the length of his chains and crashed back down to the floor, snarling.

Cade ignored the outburst, trying to keep the creature from focusing on its hunger.

"Do you know where they are, George?"

Winston snarled and snapped at Cade with his rotting teeth, his control uncertain.

Cade tried again. "Help me find them, George. Tell me where they've gone. Help me get the ones who did this to you."

Winston didn't respond, just went back to staring at the flesh in Cade's hand.

"You've got to tell me more, George. I need your help. Do you know where they are?"

Nothing.

"Come on, George. Don't stop now."

Still nothing.

Just that stare.

And the hunger it conveyed.

Realizing that he would get nothing further from the revenant until it had fed again, Cade tossed him the thin strip of flesh.

Like a rabid dog, the creature threw itself onto the morsel, its eyes alight with an unholy hunger.

But as Winston raised the meat to his lips, he suddenly froze in mid-motion, his hand halfway to his mouth.

He stayed that way for several long moments.

Cade signaled for the others to hold still. As they watched, the former Templar shook his head violently, like a dog shaking itself free of water. He slowly lowered the hand holding the morsel to his side and mumbled something further.

Moving slowly, Cade crouched so that he was on the same level as the revenant. "What did you say, George?"

Again, the same garbled phrase.

Impatiently, Cade moved closer. In the next room, Olsen and Riley both went on alert, but didn't interfere with their commander.

"Please, George. One more time."

Winston repeated his statement and this time, Cade understood. What he had first taken for gibberish was actually a two-word phrase, repeated frantically over and over again several times.

"Help me."

Cade stared into the other man's eyes and saw hope there.

For what seemed like the longest time neither man moved.

Then, in one swift motion, Cade drew his gun and shot the former Templar in the head.

The revenant's body crashed to the floor, unmoving, his gaze now fixed permanently on the wall behind him.

As the Father Garcon stepped forward and began blessing the body, Cade stood, whispered a gentle, "Godspeed," and turned away.

He had a nest of necromancers to find.

# CHAPTER 13

T HEY SPENT THE REST OF that day and the majority of the next wading through database after database in an effort to correlate the scant leads they had against lists of known enemies of the Order. The initial threat assessment had come back with over four hundred groups or individuals who had reason to want to harm the Order, from rival religious groups to magickal societies that openly worshipped the devil. From there they had begun the process of correlating the list of names with other known facts, such as the ability to raise a revenant, proximity to the locations of the attacks, and any connection they could find with the number nine.

By early evening, they still had way too many possibilities to contend with. It was going to be a long night.

They needed more information, more details to help narrow the search.

The hoped-for forensic results came back from Ravensgate late the next day, but ultimately proved unhelpful, confirming only what they already knew - that some person or persons unknown had assaulted the compound, murdered everyone on the grounds without the use of modern weaponry, then disappeared back into the night without a trace.

The team was getting frustrated, the long hours of research without anything to show for it wearing at their nerves.

They needed something else to happen if they were going to make any progress.

In the early hours of their third day at Folkenberg, something did.

Just after 3 A.M., Captain Stanton sent word that the Broadmoor commandery in upstate New York had just been attacked. This time, with the troops on full alert, they were able to repel the attackers after a fierce firefight. According to the base commander, they had a lot of information for Commander Williams.

The plane was fueled and the team's equipment loaded. With thanks to Captain Stanton and his men, Echo Team departed just as the sun was coming up over the horizon.

\* \* \*

A car and driver was waiting for them when they arrived in Syracuse just over an hour and a half later. They passed the ride in silence, not wanting to talk about the investigation in front of a stranger, fellow Templar or not, the suspicion of an inside ally still prominent in their thoughts.

They were met at the gate by the acting commander, Major Barnes, who led them onto the property and explained what his men had encountered during the battle the evening before. He told a harrowing tale of a wall of fog that enveloped the grounds, of spectral creatures that hunted in its depths. He told of their frantic efforts to throw back the invaders, only to be beaten time and time again. He summed things up with a look of disgust. "By the time it was over, we had thirty-five men dead, sixty-seven wounded. And all we have to show for our efforts was a single corpse."

Cade gave the man his full attention. "One of theirs?"

"Yeah. Somebody made a lucky shot, it seems. We're not sure why, but shortly after he was killed the fog dissipated, and the attack faded away to nothing."

Cade felt his excitement growing. "Let's have a look at that body."

The corpse had been left where it had fallen, some hundred yards away from the entry in the open grass. The man had been in his early thirties, with long black hair and a well-kept beard. He was dressed in a thick robe complete with a hood, something that looked like it belonged in the Middle Ages, beneath which he wore a T-shirt and jeans. The bullet wound in his chest told the rest of the story.

But it was the signet ring on his left hand that drew Cade's attention.

A ring with a skeletal snake chasing its own tail surrounding the number nine.

Known as the Ouroboros, the snake symbolized many things in many cultures: the circular nature of life, the cyclical power of the universe, the idea that all things are renewed through entropy and decay.

He had no idea what the nine represented, but at least he know understood why Winston had been focused on the number.

Cade knew that he was looking at his first concrete clue to the attackers' identities.

Assuming that the dead man had been the sorcerer who had summoned the ghostly fog, it seemed logical to guess that his death had banished the creatures back to their own realm of existence.

Around them, Barnes's men were hard at work collecting the bodies of the dead, both those that had perished at the hands of the Enemy and those that had risen again only to be sent on to their final rest by their fellow Knights. It was a gruesome sight, one that filled Cade with unease, for he knew that he could have been investigating another deserted commandery if Barnes's troops had not succeeded in repelling the assault. The thought prompted a question.

Turning back to the major, Cade asked, "Any idea what their objective was?"

"We're not entirely certain. As near as I can tell, the attack was a diversion, designed to hide whatever it was that they were doing in the cemetery. We found a block and tackle set up over a grave, but we haven't had time to look into it further yet."

"Show me," said Cade.

Barnes led them across the property and into the cemetery. It was a large one, with graves dating back more than one hundred years, yet the one they finally stopped at wasn't more than a year old. The inscription read simply JULIUS SPENCER, 1944-2003." The coffin had been dug out of the grave and its lid torn open, but the body of the former Knight remained resting peacefully inside. The aforementioned block and tackle lay discarded in the grass a few feet away. Unlike the scene at Templeton, with its many desecrated graves, here only this particular one had been disturbed.

As Riley questioned the locals for more details, Cade stepped away from the others and used his Sight to survey the scene around him

With it he could see that the graveyard existed in the Beyond, just as it did here, but that was where the similarity ended. In the real world, the graveyard was a well-manicured place of respect and remembrance. In the Beyond, it was a wild, desolate locale.

The grass was overgrown, knee high in most places, obscuring many of the gravestones. The stones themselves were cracked and worn, the writing on their surfaces obscured by overgrowths of fungi and mold. The trees, in the real world lush and healthy, were disease-ridden hulks in the Beyond, their leafless branches stretching down almost to the ground, their skeletal forms stark against the grey sky. Off to his left, the brooding form of the manor house stood watch in the distance.

A flicker of motion caught his eye.

When he turned to find it, he saw a shadowy figure standing out among the gravestones. Before he could get a good look, the figure moved off, disappearing from view among the markers.

He suspected he knew the spirit's identity, however.

Later, he would verify that suspicion.

*It was time they found some answers to this puzzle.*

# CHAPTER 14

AFTER ORDERING HIS MEN TO get some rest, Cade retired to his own room, ostensibly to do the same. In truth the Commander had much different plans.

Once inside, he closed his bedroom door but left it unlocked. Moving into the bathroom, he took the mirror down off the wall and returned with it to the bedroom, placing it flat on the floor next to the bed. He took a pad of paper out of the desk, wrote a short note to Riley explaining what he intended to do, and placed the note prominently on his pillow.

He left both of his guns in his kit bag; firearms didn't work in the Beyond. While he didn't exactly understand why, he had come to the conclusion it had something to do with the fact that the spiritual nature of the place didn't mesh well with the mechanical nature of the gun itself. This seemed to be supported by the fact that melee weapons, powered only by the strength and determination of the wielder, worked without a problem. In fact, the more emotional the attacker, the more damage the blow inflicted.

Cade knelt on the prie dieu that stood in the corner of his

room and took a few moments to prepare himself mentally for his journey across the barrier. Reaching the other side was always a difficult and draining task. Without a clear head, he could end up getting lost or not having the strength to make the return journey.

The Beyond was still very much a mystery to Cade, despite his many journeys there. As nearly as he could tell, it was a shadow realm that existed close to the real world in time and space, but forever separated by a wall of energy he had come to call the barrier. Like the mystical Purgatory, it was inhabited by the shades of the dead, those that for one reason or another had not moved on to a more lasting rest. Other creatures inhabited the Beyond as well, dark, twisted creatures that hunted the shades and roamed the land in great predatory packs. For lack of a better name, Cade called them spectres, after the mythical creatures of legend. He avoided them wherever and whenever he could.

The fact that Spencer's spirit remained in the area around his grave told Cade that he would probably find the former Templar close by on the other side of the barrier. Cade intended to make the crossing with the hope of contacting Spencer's shade and finding out just what made him so interesting to the opposition.

Cade strapped his sword across his back in its habitual carry position and moved to the other side of the bed.

Without further delay, he stepped through the surface of the mirror.

* * *

The squad members were assigned to guest rooms in the east wing of the house, identical to Cade's. The rooms were small, with a minimum of furnishings; a narrow bed, a desk and chair, and a kneeler in the corner for prayer time. A small bathroom, containing a toilet, sink, and mirror, was connected to each room.

The events of the last twenty-four hours had worn Olsen out, and he intended to get some rest while he had the chance. Rack time was a sparse commodity in Cade's unit, and who knew when they would be called out again? He placed his computer equipment on the nearby desk and hung his gun off the edge of the headboard, where it would be within easy reach.

As a final preparation before sleeping, Olsen stripped the pillow case from the pillow and took it into the bathroom. There he took the mirror down off the wall, placed it inside the pillow case, and then remounted the mirror facing backward. He smiled at the thought of the rumors that would fly if they left them that way and the locals found all of the mirrors in the rooms used by Echo Team covered up in such a fashion, but he knew it wouldn't happen. The team was very cautious about protecting their commander's secrets.

Olsen turned out the lights, stretched out on the bed, and tried to get some sleep.

Unfortunately, sleep was more elusive than he hoped.

He'd reached that stage of being so overtired that his mind refused to shut down. It was still working at the problem of whom or what they were facing, and worrying the issue like a dog with a bone. *Some research might be just what he needed.*

He brought his laptop over to the bed and fired it up. As he'd expected, the room itself did not contain any ports with which to plug into the Order's servers; those were reserved for the library and research areas, the better to monitor what individual Knights were doing online. But that hadn't hampered his net-based activities in quite some time. *It's amazing what a little knowledge and a properly configured wireless network card can do.*

Five minutes later he was clandestinely disguised as an authorized net spider and roaming through the Order's personnel records. He started with the name on the grave they'd visited earlier.

It didn't take him long to find Spencer's records. He went through the man's personal history, noting his middle-class background and advanced education. He'd spent time in the armed forces before being recruited to join the Order.

Olsen next turned his attention to the list of duty assignments, looking for anything out of place, anything unusual that might have caused the attackers to single out Spencer's grave from all the others in the cemetery.

One notation in particular caught his eye.

Olsen stared at it, thinking, then he got up, left his room, and walked down the hallway past several doors until he came to the room to which Riley had been assigned. He knocked softly on the door.

No answer.

He knocked again, louder this time. When still he received no response, he calmly began pounding on the door as hard as he could. He kept it up until he heard the snap of the lock on the other side.

Riley partially opened the door and stared out at Nick.

"Tell me why I shouldn't kill you where you stand, Olsen," the big man said.

Nick ignored him. "You spent time at the Birmingham commandery before joining Echo, didn't you?"

Riley continued to stare. "This can't wait until morning?"

"No. Answer the question."

Sighing, Riley said, "Yeah. Three years. It was hot and humid, and that was the best part of the assignment."

Nick headed back toward his own room. "Come here and check this out. I think we've got a problem."

Riley disappeared back inside his room, then emerged again a few moments later, fully dressed. He strode down the hall to Nick's room and peered over his shoulder as he brought up Spencer's personnel records. The man's service record and photograph appeared on the screen.

"Recognize him?"

Riley took a good, long look. "No. Should I?"

"Yes." Olsen frowned. "You both supposedly served in Birmingham at the same time." Riley had a near-photographic memory for faces and names. According to the records, Spencer had served five years at the Birmingham commandery. During that time the two men would have had to have run into each other at some point. Even if they were assigned to opposite shifts of duty, they would have seen each other while off duty or during worship times. The commandery in Birmingham just wasn't that big.

Olsen dug a little deeper into the records.

* * *

The landscape of the Beyond was constantly shifting, like a fun house mirror, hauntingly familiar yet intimately strange. Sometimes it was vastly different from where he had entered the rift; other times it was as alike as a photograph and its negative.

Tonight it was the latter.

The commandery in which he emerged was a mirror

reflection of the one he had just left, though with one major difference. Here the inevitable passage of entropy was clearly visible; like a canvas painted with depression and pain, everything was hung with a patina of decay. Dark stains covered walls that seeped a foul-smelling sweat, while thick cobwebs and layers of dust hid the ceiling from view. The scent of mold hung heavily in the air. Underneath the mold, other less identifiable but equally unpleasant odors lingered. Great gaping holes littered the floor of the hallway. Through them he could see the floor below and. in one notable case, all the way to the basement deep beneath the house.

He cautiously descended the stairs, expecting them to collapse beneath him at any moment, and was finally able to reach the ground floor without mishap after several slow, agonizing minutes. From there he quickly made his way to the front door and out into the night.

He set off across the lawn, moving toward the graveyard on the far edge of the estate, just as he had earlier in the day. Where in the real world the grass was vibrantly green, here it was limp and lifeless. And like everything else in the Beyond, it was one of a thousand subtle shades of grey. Great burrow-like holes littered the area, displaying tunnels that disappeared into the dank earth below, tunnels that seemed to devour even the scant light cast by the feeble stars above.

Cade didn't like their looks and made wide, sweeping detours to avoid them.

It was a long walk, longer than he remembered and therefore suspect in the constantly shifting landscape, though at last he came to the cemetery. The waist-high gate of iron that guarded the entrance in the real world had been torn down, but here in the Beyond it still hung on its rusted frame.

Cade moved through the gate onto the cemetery grounds.

In the living world the grave markers were carefully tended; here, many of them were split in two. Their top halves lay discarded and forgotten in the uncut grass, their bottom portions caked with strange growths and odd lichens that obscured the inscriptions. The sickly light of a waning moon cast shadows across the scene, shadows that seemed to weave and dance around him.

A sudden motion out of the corner of his eye caught his attention. Reacting on instinct, Cade spun to his left.

The blade that should have severed his arm at the shoulder merely nicked his skin as he turned. A dark, barely glimpsed figure dashed past him and disappeared behind a nearby mausoleum.

Cade called after the departing figure. "I mean you no harm." He spoke in Latin, the universal language of the Order. Despite his statement he drew his own sword, so he would be ready to defend himself if and where necessary. There was no telling how the other would react to his intrusion into the Beyond. His reception had been less than welcome by other denizens of the place.

Cade moved closer to Spencer's grave. Twice more he was attacked. Twice more he managed to twist out of the way of the deadly weapon at the last moment. Still, he did not attempt to attack the other man in turn. He suspected the shade was Spencer, and he needed his cooperation, not his animosity.

He was also beginning to believe that the man's attacks were nothing more than a test, a challenge to his worthiness. Each time the other man had him dead to rights, yet Cade had managed to elude the killing blow.

With a confidence born of this new consideration, Cade

moved toward the figure waiting for him by the grave, a figure with a naked longsword visible in its right hand.

Cade stopped several feet away. He replaced his own sword in its sheath and let his hands fall to his side with his palms open, clearly showing his lack of hostile intent.

The two men studied each other.

Cade waited, enduring the inspection.

The silence stretched.

Finally, the other spoke.

"Why have you come here?"

The man's voice was soft but carried the hard tones of command quite clearly across the distance that separated them.

"I need your help."

The figure stared. "The living are not welcome here."

Cade ignored the implied threat. "The Order is under assault. I need to understand who is behind the attacks and what they are after. I believe you can give me the answers I need."

The former Knight turned away. "I cannot help you."

"You must!" Cade demanded. "Our brothers are dying. Our dead are being ripped from their graves, forced to walk the earth. You know who is behind this. You must help us." His shout echoed across the desolate landscape.

The shade continued to walk away.

"By your Vow, by your pledge to the Lord, I demand that you honor my request. *Let each, as well as he can, bear another's burdens, so that one may honor another.*"

"Do not quote the Rule to me!" the dead Knight answered angrily, spinning around to face Cade again. "You do not know what it is like to wander this place. You don't know the unrest, the yearning for finality that I have endured since coming here. You do not know the horrors that I have seen! After my faithful service, I am reduced to this? You should bear *my* burdens."

But Cade would not be deterred. "If my taking your place could save the lives of those in my care, then I would be the first to volunteer. But I don't have that option. If not for the Order, then do it for your brother soldiers, those who fought and died in the name of the cause as earnestly as you did. They believed. They gave their lives willingly. Don't let their sacrifices be in vain. Don't let their rest be shattered in the way that your own has. With your help I can stop this, I know I can."

For a moment, Cade thought he had failed. The dead Templar raised his weapon, his face contorted in anger. Cade braced himself for the battle to come, but something in his earnest plea must have finally reached the other man for the blow Cade anticipated never came. The former Templar slowly lowered his weapon and nodded in defeat.

"Very well, I will help you. But you will not like what you will hear."

The man's soft, quiet statement only heightened Cade's curiosity.

# CHAPTER 15

THIS IS INTERESTING," OLSEN SAID, pointing to a particular line on the screen.

"A training assignment? We all have those. So what?"

"One that lasted two years?"

Riley frowned and looked closer at the screen. "Two years? That doesn't make any sense." Both men knew that such assignments rarely, if ever, lasted more than six months. If you couldn't cut it in your new unit in that time frame, you were transferred elsewhere. "Is there any more information?"

When Olsen tried to access the detailed information, he struck a command prompt that asked for a user ID and password. He plugged in his standard codes, fully expecting to gain access, only to be bumped back out again with an error message that informed him that the information he was trying to reach was classified.

"What the . . .?" Olsen thought for a moment, then inserted a second set of codes.

The classified warning blinked back at them from the screen

for a second time.

"Try mine." When that, too, failed to work, Riley said, "So much for that."

But his partner shook his head. "We're not finished yet." When the prompt came up a third time, Olsen inserted Cade's personal codes.

"The commander would have your scalp if he knew you had his codes." Riley said ominously.

Olsen grinned. "I know. That's why we aren't going to tell him, right?"

He received a smile in return. "Mum's the word."

But once again, the security system kicked them out.

Olsen was frustrated, but by no means beaten. He had an ace up his sleeve for defeating the system security, but he was holding it in reserve, until he was certain they were on to something. For the moment, Echo Team's security expert decided to take another route. He called up a list of the commanderies that had suffered assaults in the last several days. Then he accessed the property records for each, creating a list of all of the Order's members who had been interred at the cemeteries on those sites. He then instructed the computer to hunt through the service records for those individuals, flagging every member who had a long-duration training assignment similar to Spencer's.

Ten minutes later the computer spit back a list of five names. Each and every one of them had been assigned to Birmingham for the same training assignment. But when Olsen tried to dig deeper into the individual records, he received the same results. Any detailed information regarding those assignments was classified. And Riley, assigned to the same location during the same time period, didn't recognize any of the names on the list.

His suspicions growing, Riley said, "Can you check that assignment against the service records of the entire Order, using today's date?"

"Why?"

"I want to see how many other men there are and where they're located now."

Olsen considered the request. "That kind of search might set off a few alarms."

"The system thinks you're Cade. What do you care?"

"Good enough for me." Olsen set the process in motion, then sat back to wait for the results.

The two men talked over various theories regarding the attacks in the half hour it took for the computer to complete its task. When it had, they were faced with a list of twenty names.

Every one of them was assigned to the Preceptor's commandery in Bristol, Rhode Island.

None of them were familiar to either of the Echo Team members.

Olsen tried to use Cade's pass codes to access the individual records and learn more, but even that gambit failed. He was not to be deterred, however; he had the sense that he had a major piece of the puzzle right in front of him if he only had the wherewithal to follow it to its source, and he fully intended to do just that. It was time to use his ace in the hole. "I've been saving this for a real emergency. Something tells me this is one," he said.

Early in his relationship with the Order, Olsen had been assigned to the unit in charge of developing the Templar technological infrastructure. During that time, he had used his knowledge of network systems to bury a back door deep behind the security systems, a hidden port of entry into the heart of the

Order's framework. It could only be used once, but when it was, it allowed Olsen to roam around the system as a root administrator with complete access to all but the most fortified sections of the database.

With the help of the back door and a slick little utility that masqueraded as an authorized net spider, Olsen broke through.

An entire unit was hidden there.

Neither of the men had been aware of its existence, and they pored over the information with a great degree of shock and surprise. What they had in front of them was a standard TO&E. The Table of Organization and Equipment was a document that identified the unit's rank structure, mission, and arms and equipment. This particular unit was identified as the *Custodes Veritatis*, or Guardians of Truth.

From what they could determine, its primary mission was to protect and preserve the Holy Relics that the Order had obtained over the years, everything from Veronica's Veil to the staff of Moses. Knight Commander Nigel Stone was listed as the unit commander and all twenty of the previous names they had uncovered showed up on the current duty roster. The unit's historical records showed that all five of the deceased had been members at one time or another as well.

"Who does Stone report to?" Riley asked.

A few key strokes later they had their answer.

"Son of a . . ."

"My feelings exactly," Olsen said, nodding in agreement. "The boss sure ain't gonna be happy about this."

Before Riley could reply the emergency alarms outside in the corridor began blaring.

The commandery was under attack.

The two men grabbed their weapons and rushed out into the

corridor, the computer, and the damning evidence it contained, forgotten on the desk inside.

\* \* \*

"What are they looking for?"

Cade and his companion were seated on the cracked surface of a marble sarcophagus, where they had settled after the shade of the dead Templar had finally agreed to talk.

The shade's answer was short and to the point. "The Spear of Destiny."

Cade sat back in surprise. The Spear of Destiny was the mythical name given to the lance the Roman centurion Longinus used to pierce the side of Christ while he hung on the cross, thus fulfilling the Old Testament prophecies. It was also known as the Spear of Longinus or the Lance of Mauritius. Cade knew that historically the Lance had allegedly been possessed by a series of successful military leaders including Alaric, Attila the Hun, Charlemagne, and even Hitler, all of whom claimed it was the power of the Lance that led them to victory.

"Why do they want it?"

Spencer simply looked at him, not bothering to respond.

The Templar Commander realized the futility of his question. Reviewing what he knew about the Lance, the why of it all quickly became obvious. There was a legend that whoever possessed the weapon would be able to conquer the world. Napoleon attempted to obtain the Lance after the Battle of Austerlitz, but it had been smuggled out of the city prior to the start of the fight, and he never got hold of it. Charlemagne carried the Spear through forty-seven successful battles, but died when he accidentally dropped it. Barbarossa met the same fate only a few minutes after it slipped out of his hands while he was crossing a stream.

The modern history of the Spear wasn't as well documented. Somehow it eventually wound up in the possession of the House of the Hapsburg and was placed in the Hoffberg Treasure House in 1912, where Hitler was later to "discover" it. A rabid student of the occult and fully aware of the legend attached to it, Hitler had the Spear moved to St. Catherine's Church in Berlin shortly after he came to power. As the Americans and Russians advanced on Berlin, he had it moved again, this time to an underground bunker to protect it from Allied bombing raids. That bunker fell to the U.S. on April 30, 1945, and an Army officer took possession of the weapon. Consistent with the legend, Hitler committed suicide in his bunker just eighty hours after he lost control of the Spear. General Patton was particularly interested in the weapon and took the time to have its authenticity traced. His fanaticism on the subject was eventually brought to Eisenhower's attention, however, who found the whole subject distasteful. If Cade remembered correctly, it was Eisenhower who returned the Lance to its rightful location, the Hofberg Treasure House in Vienna, where it was supposedly still on display.

*If the legends are true, and the Necromancer and his allies gain control of the weapon, we've got a much bigger problem on our hands.*

But one issue kept nagging at him. He seemed to remember both the Hoffberg Museum and the Vatican itself claimed to control the real Lance. If that was true, why was the Council of Nine attacking Templar commanderies looking for the weapon?

He put the question to Spencer.

The answer was not what he had expected. "Because the

Council knows that for the last fifty years it has rested in a vault controlled by a secret unit within our own Order."

Cade sat there, stunned by the reply.

# CHAPTER 16

D UNCAN WAS ASLEEP WHEN THE emergency alarms sounded but was out of bed and ready within seconds. Weapons in hand, he rushed from his bedroom just in time to join Olsen and Riley as they emerged from Cade's room across the hall.

"The Knight Commander?" he asked, as the three of them rushed down the way.

"Not in his room," was Riley's quick answer, and his tone conveyed both his concern and his suggestion to let the matter drop.

The three of them dashed down the stairs and emerged in the grand foyer, just in time to meet a group of revenants as they crashed through the front door.

The Knights moved as one, splitting into a V-shaped formation. Riley took point with Duncan on his left and Olsen on his right. Without hesitation, the master sergeant opened up on the intruders with his automatic weapon, his companions' fire joining the fray only a split second later.

The revenants never stood a chance. Caught in the

concentrated fire of the three Knights, the creatures were quickly cut to ribbons.

The three men waded through the bodies, dispatching any that they found with life left in them with a quick gunshot to the head, and took up positions facing out the open doorway.

What they saw outside momentarily took their breath away.

The front lawn was literally crawling with revenants. It was as if the doors of hell had suddenly been opened.

\* \* \*

Cade emerged from the Beyond to find himself in an unused room on the second floor of the Broadmoor commandery. As always, the mirror he used as an exit point shattered violently with his passage, and he paused for a moment, waiting to see if anyone would come to investigate the sound of breaking glass.

He needn't have bothered. The warbling tones of the emergency alarms sounding in the corridors would have masked the sound easily.

The sound of gunfire reached him the moment he stepped out of the room. He listened for a moment, trying to pinpoint its location. As best he could tell it was coming from somewhere out in front of the commandery. He moved down the hallway until he reached a window. His viewpoint gave onto the front entrance to the manor house and the grounds beyond, meaning that Cade was in the east wing, exactly opposite where he had started.

In the light of the floodlights that were mounted on the roof, Cade could see revenants dashing across the lawn, only to be thrown back or brought down by the concentrated firepower of the Knights guarding the front entrance. The front gate lay in ruins, and more revenants poured through the gap even as he watched. Several could be seen gorging themselves on the corpses of those who had defended the gate, next to the smoking ruin of the security shack.

The missing men from the Templeton commandery had come home.

Despite the fact that he was unarmed, Cade never hesitated. He turned and ran for the stairs at the other end of the hall, intent on joining the fray.

As he moved, the flicker of light caught his eye.

A portal had formed in the middle of the front lawn, a silver mirror-like disk of shimmering power some ten feet across. Its surface rippled and swirled, as if something was disturbing it from below.

Cade dashed down the hall and stepped out through a set of French doors. He found himself on a balcony over the portico that guarded the entrance to the manor house. A group of Knights were crouched behind the low wall that ran around the balcony's edge, firing everything they had at the portal below.

Cade was just in time to witness to the birth of a nightmare as it dragged itself through the gateway and into this world.

A hand came first, a hand the size of a small horse, twisted and gnarled, the color of melting lead. It was four-fingered, and each finger ended in a vicious claw. The hand was joined by another, this one on the other side of the portal. Its fingers grasped the edge of the lawn, and the creature slowly pulled itself into view.

Cade faltered to a halt as he stared in dismay at the demon.

It stood well over twenty feet tall and was humanoid in appearance. Its skin was the color of a pig left too long on the roasting spit, deep crimson and black, and it glistened wetly in the floodlights. Its head was misshapen, like wax that had rested too close to a fire, and four large bulbous eyes stared lustfully at the world around it from within the depths of what could only charitably be called a face.

As he watched, a group of Templar defenders emerged from around the corner of the west wing and began firing at it. In reply it reached out, grasped a nearby Suburban in one large fist and hurled it at the Knights, silencing their counterattack with one blow.

Cade ran to the wall and looked out over the field of battle, knowing he had little time to find what he needed.

*All right you son of a bitch, where are you?*

He looked beyond the oncoming beast, searching for a spot back from the center of the fray in a place of reasonable safety. He strained to see through the flashes of gunfire and the glare from the spotlights on the roof above.

*There!*

A sorcerer stood beneath the sheltering branches of a large elm tree near the wall surrounding the estate. His head was bowed in concentration, and his hands moved rhythmically through the air in front of him

Having found his target, Cade glanced beside him. The nearest of Barnes's soldiers was firing shot after shot into the approaching demon with a standard-issue M14. It would have to do.

Cade grabbed the rifle from the startled soldier and rushed twenty feet farther along the parapet, shouldering the weapon in the process. He did his best to ignore both the approaching behemoth and the confusion of the soldiers around him, knowing he was unlikely to get a second shot. With the rooftop shaking beneath his feet from the creature's approach, he settled in for the shot.

The view through the scope showed his target in more detail. He was dressed exactly like the man Cade had examined earlier, right down to the robe and the ring on one hand. Cade eyeballed the distance between them as roughly 350 meters. If he'd had his own rifle and the time to study the situation and get into position, it would have been easy. But with an unfamiliar weapon, in the midst of a firefight, with a crazed demon bearing down on him at full speed, well, it was going to be interesting.

A slight breeze wafted against his cheek, and Cade made a minor adjustment to his position.

The demon moved another fifteen feet closer with a single step.

The men on the roof were firing wildly, some scrambling back from their positions, their fear at facing such a creature getting the better of them. In seconds, the organized resistance dissolved into a panicked retreat as the rest of the men realized that their gunfire was having no effect.

Cade ignored everything but the target.

*Steady,* he thought.

His attention narrowed to a pinpoint, his entire world reduced to the figure in the reticle of his scope and the voice in his ear, waiting for the green-light command and the moment when all those years of training would come together at the pull of a trigger.

The demon stepped off the grass and onto the asphalt of the driveway, less than twenty feet from where Cade perched on the rooftop.

*Breathe . . .*

He pulled the trigger.

\* \* \*

"Good Lord," breathed Duncan at the sight.

For years he'd known that the Enemy was real, that this world was home to more than just God's creations. But unlike the other members of Echo Team, who fought such supernatural creatures regularly, Duncan had been sheltered from them owing to his assignment. It was one thing to know something intellectually in the back of your mind, quite another to come face-to-face with it.

For a moment, he froze. He was unable to do anything but stare in dread at the foul creature closing the gap between them.

It was the sound of Riley's voice that jerked him out of his paralysis. The master sergeant was yelling at the top of his lungs as he fired his weapon at the demon, and the sound was enough to jerk Duncan back into action. As Olsen turned his attention to a pack of oncoming revenants, sniping away at them as they moved closer to where the three men were positioned, Duncan added his own fire to Riley's. At the same moment a torrent of gunfire suddenly began pouring into the demon from somewhere on the roof above.

Despite the sheer volume of firepower, it did no good.

The demon barely noticed the bullets slamming into its flesh. It continued moving forward, intent on reaching the manor house before it.

\* \* \*

Cade's bullet leapt from the gun and smashed into the flesh of the demon's left arm as it swung to the side in a random arc.

"Shit!"

Cade prepared to fire again, but the demon had closed in, blocking his shot at the sorcerer who had summoned it. He'd have to get higher in order to fire over the creature's shoulder.

There was only one choice.

Ignoring the fact that the demon was only scant feet away, Cade scrambled up onto the wall in front of him. He brought the weapon back up into firing position and sighted once more on his target.

He was horribly exposed, and knew it.

Yet he had no other choice.

The demon let out a blood-chilling roar at the sight of his audacity. It reached for him with one four-fingered hand, its claws gleaming in the floodlights.

The sorcerer looked up and Cade stared through the scope directly into the man's eyes.

*Good-bye*, he thought, then pulled the trigger.

At almost the same instant, the demon's gnarled hand wrapped itself around Cade's waist and yanked him off the parapet. His rifle tumbled free and fell to the ground, two stories below, as the creature began to crush the life out of him simply by squeezing its fist.

He fought against the creature's grip, but it was like punching a steel band. It was all he could do to keep air in his lungs.

The demon raised its fist higher to get a better look. Hot fetid breath washed across Cade's face, followed seconds later by the thing's unearthly laugh of triumph. Four inhuman eyes regarded Cade with glee as the demon's mouth opened wide.

\* \* \*

By the edge of the estate, the sorcerer lay on the ground,

bleeding from the chest. With a final rattling gasp, life left him. In the same instant, the portal through which the demon had been summoned suddenly reversed its flow, becoming a conduit back into the next.

It wanted its own back again.

And it would take anything else it could along with it.

\* \* \*

The demon faltered and came to a stop.

Involuntarily, it took a step backward.

Something was pulling at the creature from behind.

Reluctantly, the demon turned its attention to this new problem.

In that moment, the portal pulsed a second time and the demon was yanked off its feet from the sheer force of the suction it generated.

In surprise, the creature opened its fist.

\* \* \*

Cade fell.

His arms reached out, desperate to find purchase on something before his body smashed itself against the unforgiving ground below.

As he fell past the balcony, his fingers brushed up against the edge of the stone railing, and he instinctively grabbed at it.

With a bone-jarring impact, he managed to stop his fall.

Only to find himself hanging by his arms two stories above an enraged demon.

* * *

The rest of Echo's command unit watched in stunned amazement as the demon suddenly slammed to the ground face-first. It pushed itself up on its arms, only to fall forward again as something began to drag it slowly from behind.

Which was rather amazing, since they could see there was nothing there.

With a howl of anger, the demon tried to fight against the pull. It dug its fingers into the asphalt of the driveway. It kicked its legs. It thrashed its body side to side, crushing several revenants that got too close.

Nothing worked.

Slowly but surely, the demon continued slipping backward away from the Templars.

A baleful howl suddenly split the night air, rising swiftly in pitch like a banshee's wail until it overpowered even the sounds of gunfire still coming from above.

"What's happening?" Duncan cried over the noise.

Olsen came to his aid. "The summoner's lost control of the portal," he answered, between shots at distant revenants. "It's reversed itself. Anything that entered through it is about to go back out again in a big hurry." A grin appeared on his face. "Including that ugly son of a bitch in front of us."

Duncan suddenly found a grin of his own.

* * *

Above them, undetected by his fellow team members, Cade slowly began to lose his grip on the railing.

Even if his teammates could have heard him over the noise of the enraged demon, it was doubtful that they could reach him in time, so instead of calling out he searched for some sort of foothold, something to support his weight for the fraction of a second he needed to regain his grip on the railing above.

Unfortunately, that particular section of the wall was slick with polished stone.

His left hand suddenly lost its grip.

His body twisted outward with the momentum, putting more strain on his right hand. He was turned partially toward the front gate, and the position afforded him a view of the demon as it was dragged inexorably back toward the portal.

A twisted rope of shimmering energy extended from the rapidly closing portal and across the lawn, to wrap around the demon's legs just below the knees. It pulsed and pulled in time with the shrinking opening to the portal; it wouldn't be long before the demon was hauled back to its own plane of existence, back to where it belonged.

Revenants still roamed the grounds, but the element of surprise had long since worn off, and the Knights had gained the upper hand.

This time, the Templars had won.

*Though I might not be around to celebrate*, Cade thought, as his fingers slipped another quarter inch.

Luckily, several of the retreating Knights on the balcony above had seen Cade's heroic stand and rushed back out after the danger passed to see what had become of him. Their discovery was just in time to keep him from falling to the ground two stories below.

As he was pulled up over the edge of the balcony, movement out by the front gate caught his eye. A billowing cloud of fog hung nearly ten feet in the air, throbbing and rolling in several directions at once. Cade could see faces appear and disappear within its depths, each one seeming in agony, their mouths open wide in silent screams.

A hooded figure stepped out of its depths and lifted its head to look in Cade's direction. It raised one hand as if in recognition.

The Necromancer and the Templar commander stared at each other across the distance.

A wave of cold washed across Cade's form. He knew instinctively that he was looking at the individual directly responsible for the attacks on the Templar strongholds. Here was the Enemy he sought.

He triggered his Sight.

An additional aura of crimson, grey, and black surrounded the Necromancer, mixing with the grayish white shade of the sorcerer's own aura.

The sight of it made Cade's heart cry out in horrific pain.

He knew that pattern.

He didn't know how or why. He just knew instinctively what it meant.

Without ever having seen it before, Cade knew that he was looking at the mark of the Adversary.

# CHAPTER 17

I N THE AFTERMATH OF THE attack, Cade and his men caught a few moments of privacy and compared notes. Olsen explained what he and Riley had found, revealing the existence of a special unit in the Order and to whom it reported. Cade, in turn, told them about his encounter with Spencer and the shade's belief that whoever was attacking them was doing so in order to locate and retrieve the Spear of Longinus.

Things were finally starting to make some sense, though they were still no closer to uncovering the identity of those behind it all.

Now, two hours later, Cade moved throughout the first floor, stopping briefly to talk to the defenders. His very presence, normally something that made most of the men nervous, was a welcome balm to their spirit, knowing as they did that it was the Knight Commander alone who had turned the tide of battle in their favor. While he walked, Cade checked on the preparations being made, making certain they were covered in the unlikely event that the Necromancer and his allies tried again. He reassured the wounded, letting them know that the Order's medical staff would be with them as soon as possible and seeing to it that any mortally wounded soldiers were immediately removed to the infirmary.

When he was finished he moved to the second floor and did the same. Eventually, he ended up on the balcony overlooking the entrance to the manor house, watching the recovery team move across the wide patch of front lawn as they checked for any revenants that might still be alive. An occasional gunshot punctuated their work, as they sent their former comrades off to their rest.

Cade's cell phone rang.

Still intent on watching the recovery team, he absentmindedly removed it from his belt and answered the call. "Williams."

"Commander Cade Williams?"

The voice was British and not one he recognized.

Cade went instantly on alert. His phone was unlisted; no one but the senior Templar commanders and his own sergeants knew he could be reached at this number.

Cade chose to answer with a question of his own. "Who is this?"

"My name is Nigel Stone. Can I assume I am speaking with Knight Commander Williams?"

"Yes, this is Williams. Now who are you, what do you want, and how did you get this number?"

Stone chuckled. "Easy, Commander. I'll be happy to answer your questions but one at a time please. First, are you alone?"

Williams looked around. There were several men on the observation deck with him, but all were far enough away to be out of earshot.

"I'm alone."

"Good. As I mentioned, my name is Nigel Stone. Knight

Commander Stone, to be precise. My compliments to your Sergeant Olsen. Very few individuals have ever managed to penetrate the security around my unit."

Connections were suddenly made. "You're the head of the *Custodes Veritatis*."

"Correct. And I think it is time we talked."

It was Cade's turn to laugh. "You've got that right. It's a dangerous game you're playing, you realize, especially if your unit is the target of these attacks."

Stone ignored Cade's thinly veiled threat. "Rather than have you continue to rout through our files, I thought it might be best to share what we know to date and work together on this."

"I'm listening," Cade replied.

"Not on the phone. I would prefer to meet face-to-face. While we still remain one step ahead of our attackers, they are closing the gap, and I'm concerned our security may be breached."

Cade considered that for a few moments. "Why?" he finally asked. "What do you know that I don't?"

"As I said, I'd prefer to discuss this in person. Are you familiar with Otter Lake?"

"Yes." It was a small mountain town north of Utica, about three hours drive from the Broadmoor commandery where Cade was.

Stone gave him an address. "I'll meet you there at six this evening. I'll expect you, and possibly one of your squad members, but no one else. If I see you've ignored my instructions, I'll be gone, and you'll be back to square one."

Cade chuckled ironically. "What's the matter, Stone? Don't you trust me?"

The other man's answer was sobering.

"Right now, I don't trust anyone."

Cade was left listening to a dial tone and wondering just how deep the corruption ran.

* * *

Two hours later Cade made excuses to the local commander and set off for Otter Lake. He'd made the decision to take Duncan along with him to the meeting. Olsen and Riley would remain nearby, sequestered in a local motel in case they got into trouble. For all he knew Stone could be behind it all, and Cade wanted his men close by just in case.

He signed two black Ford Expeditions out of the motor pool, and the squad split up. They traveled north until Albany, then headed west. Just past Utica they left the four-lane highway behind in favor of a two-lane state road that would take them up into the Adirondack Mountains to Otter Lake.

Otter Lake was a small mountain community that was home to less than five hundred residents in the summer and considerably less during the hard winter months. It was on Route 28, a road notorious for its impassability in the midst of winter storms. And as luck would have it, the rain began pounding against their windows halfway through the trip.

A few miles south of their destination they began looking for a motel. It didn't take long to find one that would suit their purposes; a central lodge surrounded by individual cabins just off the main stretch of road. A neon sign blinked VACANCY, and Cade turned into the parking lot. It was close enough that Olsen and Riley could be counted on to reach them quickly in an emergency.

The four of them assembled at the table in the common room of the cabin they were assigned.

Cade went over the plan one last time. "I don't expect to be gone more than an hour, two at the most. If you don't hear from us by eight o'clock, assume that something went wrong. Get some backup from Major Barnes and come on in after us. If things go completely to shit, you're going to need to go to Bristol and confront Michaels. Make him tell you where the Lance is and what he intends to do to protect it. Threaten him if you must. Do whatever you have to, but don't let that weapon fall into the enemy's hands, or we're all up shit creek. That's an order. Understood?"

The two sergeants nodded in agreement.

Cade took a few moments to study the local map Olsen had snagged from the hotel clerk, then was ready to go.

The map showed that the address Nigel Stone had given them was only another fifteen miles farther north of their position, but the winding road and bad weather forced them to go slowly and kept their pace to a minimum. As Cade drove, Duncan double-checked both of their MP5s and made certain they had ample ammunition.

The house was a newly built two-story structure with a stucco-and-fieldstone facing. Several arched windows, decorated with lintels and set in wide majestic gables, looked out onto the front lawn.

Cade stepped up and rang the bell.

When no one answered, Cade tried the door.

At the touch of his hand, it swung open slowly.

He and Duncan looked at each other.

An unspoken signal passed between them.

Guns in hand, the two men stepped across the threshold. They entered a brilliantly lit entry, its ceiling soaring eighteen feet overhead. The silence hung heavy about the place, as if it had been deserted for some time.

Room by room, they made their way through the house. The first floor held a master bedroom and bath, a kitchen, dining room, family room, and a guest room. A wide central staircase led to the second floor. There an L-shaped corridor bisected the floor, giving way to the upper portion of the family room from the first floor, two more bedrooms, and another bath.

*At the end of a long hallway was a study.*

*It was there that they found Stone.*

*He was naked, tied to a straight-backed chair in the center of the room. Wide gaping holes had been gouged into his chest, legs, and arms. He hadn't been dead for long.*

*"Shit!" Cade swore.*

*Duncan could only stare in stunned disbelief.* To have come so close . . .

*But Cade was not to be deterred. "Fuck this!" he exclaimed loudly and stepped up close to the corpse, pulling off his gloves as he did so.*

*Divining his commander's intentions, Duncan said, "I'm not certain that's such a good idea." The memory of Cade's teeth clamped leechlike on his right arm was still very much in the forefront of his mind.*

*"We don't have any other choice. If we know what happened, we have a chance of staying ahead of the game. This is the only way of getting that information."*

*"But what happens if you lose control, like you did in the cemetery?"*

*Cade's answer was matter-of-fact. "Shoot me."*

*Duncan struggled to come up with a response.*

*Without waiting for his answer, Cade grasped the hands of the corpse on the chair before him.*

A fireplace, then a small watercolor of snowcapped mountains.

The painting is lifted off the wall, and a small piece of paper is taped to its back.

Darkness.

A face hidden in the shadows of a cowled robe.

"Where is the Spear?" it asks.

Something small and vicious is half-hidden in the robed one's cupped hands.

The pair move closer and the beast, all teeth, claws, and glistening yellow eyes, is deposited on the bare skin of Stone's stomach.

As if on cue, the creature begins tunneling into his flesh.

Another set of teeth join the first. They tear at the hole the first creature made, widening it.

His vision wavering in the pain, he forces himself to look down.

His daughter, dead and buried for more than eleven years, grins up at him as her teeth find the edge of his exposed intestine, and she begins to devour it.

\* \* \*

*Cade staggered away from the corpse, his stomach churning. The sensations and memories he'd just witnessed surged in the forefront of his mind, seeking to swamp his hold on reality, but he fought them back down and buried them in their own little dark corner in the cellar of his mind. He let his anger at what the Enemy had done to his brother Knight cleanse the fog away, let it focus his attention on what needed to be done.*

*The clock was ticking, and the Enemy was still out there.*

*"Anything?" Duncan asked, from a safe position on the other side of the room.*

*Cade nodded. "He left us a note." He proceeded to describe the painting, but left out the rest of the horrific scene he'd witnessed. There were some things that only the dead should know.*

*They did a quick search of the house, finally locating the watercolor in a small storage room on the lower floor. Cade lifted it off the wall and removed the small slip of paper that had been jammed into the edge of the frame.*

*Written on it in pencil were a series of letters and numbers: B27 31 8 16.*

*"What do you think? Map coordinates?"*

*"Might also be the combination to a safe," Cade replied, "or the catalog number to a library book."*

*"There was safe in the study."*

*When they checked, they found that the safe had already been opened, however, and whatever it might have contained was long gone. Cade closed the door and spun the dial, then checked the numbers from the paper against it.*

*The door remained firmly shut.*

*"Okay, that's one possibility down. Only a couple thousand more to go," he said, with a rueful grin. Moving to the telephone sitting on a stand across the room, he called Riley and filled him in on what had occurred. He asked him to report Stone's death to Major Barnes and request that a recovery team be sent to the house as soon as possible. After agreeing to meet back at the hotel in twenty minutes, he hung up.*

*"All right. We've done all we can here. Let's regroup with the others."*

*The two men descended to the ground floor and headed for*

*the front door.*

*Just outside, they found five black-robed figures standing between them and their vehicle.*

# CHAPTER 18

I N THE NAME OF THE Lord Almighty, I call upon you to relinquish your weapons and receive the mercy of Christ the King."

Since the time of the Crusades, the Templar Rule has required that all enemies be given the chance to surrender and accept the divine grace of the Lord before hostilities can commence. Knowing what a stickler for such things Duncan seemed to be, Cade was not surprised to hear him give voice to the ritual challenge.

Even less surprising was the response the call received.

As one, the five sorcerers, dressed identically to the one Major Barnes' men had slain back at the Broadmoor commandery, raised their arms. Their leader began chanting in some ancient tongue, while the others began to weave their hands rhythmically through the air.

Duncan, apparently, had had enough for one day. "You have five seconds to surrender, or I'll open fire." His voice was steady, and he punctuated his statement by pointing his gun in their direction.

Watching all this, Cade knew Duncan's efforts were in vain. The sorcerers had baited their trap; he and Duncan had unwittingly fallen into it. As he drew his own weapon, he triggered his Sight.

The sudden link to the Beyond allowed him to see the blue witchfire that sprang forth with each motion of the sorcerers' hands, the power gathering in a rapidly growing sphere that shimmered just before them.

Cade watched as a rift appeared in the air between him and that spherical shield. It hung several feet off the ground, a small ball of incandescence that quickly began to grow and spread. From its silvery green surface a clawed hand appeared, a hand that was soon followed by an arm that grasped the edge of the opening like a physical thing and pulled the rest of its body through.

The spectre's face was hideous, a twisted parody of a human visage, warped by whatever evil passions consumed the creature. As its eyes came to rest on Cade it grinned, revealing rows of needle-sharp teeth and a spiked tongue.

Behind it, several others began to pour forth to join their brethren.

Despite the fact that they didn't have the same solidity of form that a revenant had, the spectres were actually more dangerous. Their wraithlike forms could cause just as much, if not more, harm than the rotting body of a revenant, and had the added advantage of being impervious to almost all ordinary weaponry. They were creatures of spirit and will, manifestations of pure evil, and so weapons unconnected to the emotion of the wielder could do them little harm. It took something blessed to really affect them, and, even then, several strikes were required before they were completely taken out of the picture.

Cade knew that Duncan couldn't see the mystical shield the sorcerers had created to protect themselves, but the portal and its inhabitants were clearly visible. As Cade watched, Duncan sprung into action, opening fire with his MP5.

Unfortunately, Duncan didn't have nearly the same level of experience with such beings as Cade did. He targeted the emerging spectres, and his bullets tore into the wraithlike creatures with no effect, simply passing through them to bounce off the arcane shield the sorcerers had erected.

Cade fired his own weapon, though not at the spectres. They were creatures of spirit and will, manifestations of the evil that once drove them in life, and so weapons unconnected to the emotion of the wielder could do them no harm. Instead he targeted the sorcerers summoning them, attempting to get past the barrier that they had erected to protect themselves.

His shots met the same fate as Duncan's.

The spectres swarmed about in front of the sorcerers, but made no attempt to attack the two Knights.

Cade knew the situation wouldn't remain that way for long.

Next to him, Duncan's weapon ran dry and went silent.

"Move!" Cade cried, slinging his gun and drawing his sword in preparation for the onslaught he knew was to come.

As if on cue, the spectres charged.

Duncan and Cade made it as far as the steps before the spectres burst upon them like a cyclone. Shrieking in rage and hunger, the wraithlike creatures rushed the two Knights as they turned to face their attackers at the foot of the steps, swords in hand.

Cade fought like a demon himself, snarling his fury, directing every ounce of his anger down through the weapon at his attackers. All the anger and frustration he'd felt at the sight of

Stone's mutilated body poured out of him now that he had a target. His sword spun like a dervish, striking with deadly accuracy, neither giving nor receiving any quarter from his foes. Beside him, Duncan swung his weapon with equal ferocity.

The spectres swarmed around them, striving to pierce their defenses, to gain the opportunity to sink their fangs into their flesh or rake them with their claws. At the same time, the blessed blades of the Knights sought to pierce the unnatural forms of the spectres, sending them back across the portal with a shriek of pain and a flash of witchfire every time they connected. The combination of the Knights' martial skill and the added protection of their ceramic body armor kept them from suffering any serious wounds, though they were both bleeding from half a dozen minor injuries by the time they beat back the first wave of the attack.

When the spectres pulled back to regroup, the two men quickly made their way up the steps and back inside the house, slamming the door behind them.

Cade moved to the nearest window and drew back the curtain, peering out into the front yard.

The sorcerers hadn't moved, though more spectres had emerged from the portal to join the survivors from the first wave.

"Back door," said Cade.

They ran through the lower floor, moving through the living and dining rooms, hoping they hadn't yet been surrounded. From the far side of the kitchen they could see through the sliding glass doors that led out into the patio at the rear of the house, where a seething mass of spectres pressed up against the glass from the outside, trying to force their way in.

The glass was bulging inward, the weight of the spectres proving to be too much for it. Duncan was closest to the doors when the fragile material gave way with a loud crash.

The sergeant disappeared under the onslaught.

The creatures flowed over him, coming straight for Cade.

He met them head-on, his sword flashing in the dim light.

He slashed, hacked, and stabbed, until he was once again able to beat them off. Blood flowed over his the right side of his face from a large gash at the edge of his scalp He could still see through his good eye, and that was all that mattered.

The spectres had retreated to the backyard and he glanced at them, reassuring himself they remained at a distance, before moving to assess Duncan's injuries. Cade feared the worst as he moved over to Duncan's still form, but was relieved to find he'd been knocked unconscious but was still breathing.

Kneeling next to him, his eyes on the spectres just outside the doors, Cade pulled out his radio phone and tried to call Riley, with no success.

It wouldn't be long before the spectres made another assault. He had only moments to figure a way out, or Barnes's recovery team would have two more bodies to add to their load.

But he couldn't think of a solution.

At least Riley would follow orders; when they didn't make the rendezvous, he'd head for Bristol, Olsen in tow, and confront the Preceptor. There was some small measure of comfort in that.

Then it hit him. He didn't know if it would work, but he was willing to give it a try.

"You're probably not going to like this," he said to his unconscious teammate, "but we're all out of options." Sheathing his own sword, he scooped Duncan's still form over his shoulder and grabbed the man's discarded weapon in one hand. He ran down the hall and up the steps to the second floor. He was already tired; there was no way he was going to be able to hold off another attack, not without Duncan's help.

By the time Cade made it to the end of the hall, the spectres had rallied and were in the house, swarming at the foot of the stair and climbing toward them.

Cade raced down the corridor, making for the master study where he and Duncan had found Commander Stone's remains.

The first of the spectres reached the second floor and let out a bone -chilling shriek as Cade burst into the study.

Behind him, the hallway filled with screaming wraiths.

The mirror, and the potential salvation it offered, was ten feet away.

A searing-cold hand clawed at his back, slashing partly through the back panel of his protective vest. Gritting his teeth against the pain, he dashed the final few steps across the room, planted one foot on the lip of the great mahogany desk that stood between him and the wall, and launched the two of them directly at the mirror covering the wall just beyond with one shove of his powerful legs.

*If I'm wrong, we're both dead*, he thought; and then he was gone.

# CHAPTER 19

THE TWENTY MINUTES CAME AND went.

No Cade.

Riley chalked it up to the bad weather and did his best to curb his impatience. He'd already called Major Barnes at the Broadmoor commandery and filled him in. A recovery team was on its way, with an extra squad of troops just to be safe.

Thirty minutes.

As Olsen sat watch by the window, Riley paced the small room, his frustration growing by the minute. Cade should have been here by now, rain or no rain. Something was wrong. He could feel it in his gut. He'd been Cade's right-hand man for too long just to leave him out there on his own.

By the time forty-five minutes had passed since Cade's phone call, Riley made his decision. Grabbing his shotgun off the couch, he headed for the door.

"Where are you going?" Olsen asked, from his position by the window.

"To find Cade," Riley replied, opening the door and stepping out into the darkened parking lot beyond.

Olsen grabbed his gun and followed. "'Bout damn time."

* * *

Riley pulled up to the house and both men cautiously got out of their vehicle to investigate. Olsen laid his hand on the hood of Cade's vehicle. "Cold."

"Not good."

Weapons in hand, they continued forward.

The darkness veiled both the house and yard. It wasn't until they were only a few feet away from the front door that they noticed the smashed windows and claw marks. Riley held up one hand, and both of them instantly stopped and dropped into a crouch, their eyes on the door in front of them.

Nothing moved.

Riley considered the situation. Almost an hour had passed since they'd last had contact, but that didn't mean the action was over. He remembered Cade's admonition about being a hero but discarded it. If they waited for reinforcements, it might mean life or death for Cade or Duncan if they were lying injured somewhere inside.

Riley started forward, Olsen at his back.

The search of the house went smoothly, and they didn't encounter any resistance. They found Stone's body upstairs in the study just where Cade had said it would be. In the kitchen, they found Duncan's MP5, lying in a pool of drying blood and shattered glass.

Of their teammates, Duncan and Cade, there was no sign.

Staring at the destruction around him, Riley found himself asking the same question over and over again in his mind.

*Where are you, boss?*

# CHAPTER 20

D UNCAN REGAINED CONSCIOUSNESS SLOWLY. HIS body hurt, and his mind tried to shy away from the pain, far happier to drift in a dream state than to face reality. He pulled himself to a sitting position, shaking his head to clear his thoughts.

When he finally opened his eyes, he could only stare in silent amazement at the landscape around him.

He sat amidst a patch of rocks on the shore of what appeared to be a large lake or inland sea. Small stones covered the beach, worn smooth by the water's caress. The sun was sinking out on the horizon, and its light burnished the water's surface with an unusual glow.

The incongruity of a sun setting over water on the east coast might have registered if it wasn't for the astonishing fact that everything around him was some shade of grey.

The stones.

The sky.

The water.

Even the sunlight.

All grey. A million different subtleties and shades to be sure, but grey nonetheless.

It was only when he looked down at himself that he could see some small vestiges of color, though even this was washed out and faded. His clothing, even his skin, seemed to be cast with a strange pallor, like a corpse too long in the tepid air of a newly sealed tomb.

He scrambled to his feet to get a better look around, and in doing so caught another flash of color from a nearby pile of rocks. He cautiously made his way closer.

A dark form was stretched out behind the rock, and Duncan's relief was palpable when he realized that it was Commander Williams.

Duncan rushed over to his fallen teammate.

Cade was unconscious, bruised and battered, but seemed to be without serious injury. Duncan dared not use the dark, murky water to revive him. Left with no other way to help him, he resorted to sitting by his side, waiting for Cade to regain consciousness.

It seemed to take forever.

As he sat there, a dense fog rolled in off the water, drifting in and out among the boulders that jutted out from the dark sand. He quickly realized that anything could be lurking in that fog. After what he'd already gone through, the thought made him more than a little uneasy.

When Cade did finally revive, Duncan was full of questions; questions regarding where they were, how they had arrived, and what they intended to do in order to get home.

After turning the man's sword back over to him, Cade did his best to answer them.

"Let's start with the easiest question - where we are," said

Cade. "I call it the Beyond, for lack of a better term." He explained how he had first discovered his unique ability to see into this otherworldly plane after awakening in the hospital following the attack on his family, how this led to his discovery that he had the power to walk between them. He filled Duncan in on what he knew of the place in general. Considering he'd never spoken about this with another human being, Cade thought he did an admirable job summing it all up.

Duncan, however, found his explanations anything but reassuring.

"So how did we get *here*?" he asked, looking around at the desolate landscape around them. "What happened to the portal that we came through?"

"To be honest, I've never brought anyone across with me before. Wasn't even sure I could. It's probably just simple luck that we didn't end up in the drink. As for the portal, I haven't a clue. It's probably around here somewhere."

"So you don't know where we are?"

Cade smiled grimly. "Sure I do. We're in the Beyond. I'm just not certain of our precise location."

"Lord help us!" Duncan said.

"I'm not so certain the Lord even knows this place exists," Cade replied under his breath, but would say no more on the subject when pressed for an explanation.

They spent several moments discussing what to do next. They had to find another rift, of that Cade was certain. The rifts were the only method he knew for getting back to the real world.

"So all we really need to do is find another of these portals and go back the way we came in, right?"

Cade shook his head. "I'm afraid it's a bit more complicated than that." He remembered the first time he'd come here, the wonder and amazement he'd felt. "See, every mirror in our world can potentially be used to make the journey across the barrier into the Beyond. But once here your choices become far more limited. The rifts only appear haphazardly and only for a short time. It's as if our world is spinning at a rate different from this one. When the movement of the two worlds brings a rift here in connection with a mirror there, a portal appears."

The first time, he'd slipped on his bathroom floor. Rather than smashing the mirror, his arm had passed effortlessly through the glass. A few experiments had led to his using the large mirror in the master bedroom to cross entirely to the other side. Since then, he'd been here a dozen or so times. Enough that he understood the peculiarities of travel in and out of the Beyond, but not much else. "I've seen them suddenly pop up out of nowhere and disappear just as quickly. It's one of the reasons why I never stray too far from the place where I came in. As long as I don't spend too much time here, I can safely get back out again before the portal disappears."

As he spoke he climbed wearily to his feet and began looking around, hoping to catch a glimpse of the sparkling light that was the telltale sign of a nearby portal.

Unfortunately, visibility was down to less than ten feet.

There was still more bad news to give to his companion. "So, yes, we have to find another portal. But when we do, we won't have any control over where we reenter the real world. For all we know, we could end up in the back room of a church in Moscow or in some peasant's hut in Brazil just as easily as we could end up close to where we came in. Time and distance are different here."

"But at least we'd be back in our world, where we belong," Duncan replied.

Cade couldn't argue with that.

They made the decision to follow the water's edge as a guide, hoping to come upon another portal quickly. If they did not, they could always backtrack along their path without fear of getting lost and try again in the other direction. They used a stack of small rocks to mark their starting location and prepared to set out.

That was when they noticed the eyes watching them from the fog.

"Commander?" Duncan said.

"I see them," Cade replied.

Dark, twisted shapes moved through the fog around them. For the moment they were staying back, watching and waiting; but Cade suspected that, whatever they were, they wouldn't remain there for long.

He considered their options. They could either take the fight to whatever was out there or they could head out into the water and hope the others didn't follow. One glance at the oily-looking surf let him know that wading knee deep into its depths was not something he wanted to do until absolutely necessary. Neither did charging the fog appeal to him. He didn't know exactly what was out there, but it was reasonable to assume it was dangerous, whatever it was. A benign encounter in this place was a rare thing.

But a decision was needed and he chose the least threatening one. "Start backing toward the water," Cade whispered.

Duncan nodded.

They backed up slowly, swords in hand.

The creatures, whatever they were, stayed hidden in the fog as they followed them.

As the Templars neared the water's edge, a sudden sound

reached their ears. It came from behind them, out across the water, a faint, distant splash.

"What is it?" Duncan asked, but Cade only shook his head.

From out of the fog came another splash, this time closer, and a dark, shadowy form could be seen making its way toward them. Slowly it advanced, and it soon became clear that the sound they were hearing was an oar or steering pole being dipped repeatedly into the water as the vessel drew closer.

Cade stood at the water's edge, waiting for whatever was approaching.

After a moment, Duncan moved to join him.

As the two men watched, the approaching figure finally emerged from the fog.

*Charon the Ferryman*, Cade thought, a shiver of fear striking his heart as he gazed at the newcomer. Tall and gaunt, wrapped in a long, hooded robe that prevented the two Knights from gathering any details about the visitor, the figure certainly did resemble the mystical boatman of the River Styx. The narrow boat the newcomer piloted did nothing to dispel the illusion.

For a long moment the three of them stood there, staring at each other. No one said a word. Then the ferryman lifted an arm, its hand all but hidden in the bulky folds of its sleeve, and gestured for the two soldiers to step into the boat.

"No way I'm going anywhere with that thing," Duncan said under his breath, but with the other creatures closing in on them from behind, he had little hope that they could escape under cover of the fog or fight their way through the marauding pack.

At the moment, the ferryman seemed to be their best option.

A howling cry came out of the fog behind them, mournful and hungry at the same time.

Duncan visibly started at the sound.

The figure on the boat gestured again, clearly indicating that the two of them should board the vessel before the creatures, whatever they were, found the courage to attack.

Cade moved forward and grasped the prow of the boat in one hand. The ferryman moved to the rear of the vessel, preparing to cast off and giving them room to board.

Behind Duncan, Cade could see several sets of eyes peering at them out of the fog. Misshapen forms could be seen moving closer, cutting off their escape.

"Come on!" Cade yelled.

Duncan cast one last look behind him and rushed for the boat.

The creatures chose that moment to charge.

Cade waited for Duncan to jump aboard, then pushed their boat into shallow water before clambering inside. A shrieking cry sounded right at his heels and he turned to see a wave of sinuous serpent-like forms rushing across the sand toward them, all scales and gleaming teeth.

*Too late!* his mind cried, but he had forgotten their mysterious benefactor.

The ferryman swiftly moved forward, standing over Cade where he sprawled on the floor of the boat. As the creatures closed the remaining distance to the water's edge the ferryman struck out with its staff, slashing through their forms with ease.

When the beasts retreated, the ferryman used that opportunity to take the boat out into deeper water.

Their adversaries chose not to follow.

They moved out through the shallows, headed for what Cade hoped was deeper water. The fog was thicker there. Cade quickly lost any sense of direction in the heavy, shrouding mist, but their guide moved the boat through the water with such deft precision. He was about to begin questioning their rescuer when Duncan cried out in alarm and backpedaled away from the edge of the boat.

"Sweet Jesus!"

Cade looked over the side, trying to see what had brought such an unlikely curse to his teammate's lips.

Deep within the water pale faces stared back at him, their eyes gleaming, their mouths opening hungrily, their arms stretched toward the surface as if inviting him to join them.

Cade turned away, unwilling to meet their gaze. He made several attempts to engage their guide in conversation instead, but each effort met with failure. The ferryman continued to stare straight ahead, guiding the boat on its path.

They traveled for what seemed like hours, though Cade knew that time operated differently here. Minutes could be hours, hours could be seconds; there was no direct correlation between time on this side of the barrier and time back in the living world. He and Duncan sat in the prow of the boat, holding tightly to the sides, frightened of the open water around them. Their guide remained in the stern, moving the boat across the water's surface with powerful strokes of the steering pole.

Dark clouds began to gather in the distance.

Eventually, a dark stain could be seen on the horizon. As they grew closer, details began to emerge. The black sand beach seemed to be deserted, but just above the high-tide line the shimmering surface of a rift portal could be seen hovering several feet above the ground.

A short time later their guide drove the boat through the shallows and up onto the shore. Silently he stepped out of the boat and crossed the black sand to stand before the gateway, head bowed. The wind had picked up, buffeting the two soldiers where they crouched in the gunwale of the boat, but did not seem to affect their mysterious benefactor at all.

Cade watched as the ferryman reached out and grasped the edges of the rift. With a shouted word in a harsh guttural tongue that Cade could not recognize, their benefactor suddenly wrenched the rift open wide, wide enough to let both men pass through it into the living world that was visible just beyond.

The storm flared in response. Thunder crashed in rapid succession, deafening in its majesty, and several strikes of lightning tore into the beach. The sea surged, threatening to pull the boat, and them with it, back out into the current.

Their guide waved at them with one hand.

"Let's go!" Cade yelled, over the storm.

Duncan nodded his understanding and agreement.

They climbed over the side, being careful to avoid touching the water, and fought their way up the beach against the wind until they had reached the rift. Duncan stared at its shimmering surface, the fear evident on his face. "How do we do this?" he shouted above the storm.

Cade pulled him in close. "I don't know if you can pass through the portal alone, so we'd better stay in contact. Grab my hand and hold on tight."

"What if it doesn't work?"

"Don't even think that. It *will* work."

The nervous Knight could only nod in response.

They clasped hands and stepped up close to the rift.

"Ready?" Cade yelled over the noise of the storm.

"No. But let's do it anyway."

They moved forward.

Cade's right foot pierced the shimmering surface of the rift and swiftly disappeared. A crawling sensation enveloped his leg, as if a thousand spiders had suddenly swarmed over him.

As he passed through the opening, he glanced back at their rescuer.

At that moment the wind finally succeeded in tugging their mysterious benefactor's hood to one side, revealing the face that had previously been hidden within its concealing shadows.

A face that was horribly wounded, stripped of its skin, but still recognizable.

*Gabrielle!*

They had already entered the rift. It was too late to go back; the vortex pulled them across, back through the barrier into the living world.

\* \* \*

They burst through the mirror on the other side, sending shattered glass in all directions, and ended up sprawled haphazardly on the hardwood floor. The bedroom they emerged into was small and clearly hadn't been used for some time; a layer of dust covered the furniture and floor, clearly visible in the silver glow of the moonlight coming in through the window. It was quiet, the only sound the occasional creak of the floorboards beneath their feet as they moved around the long-deserted room.

As Duncan struggled to clear the fuzziness from his thoughts, Cade shoved past him and rushed down the hall. Out in the corridor, Duncan saw his commander looking into room after room, an expression of anger on his face.

"What is it?" Duncan asked, suddenly nervous, looking around for some new threat.

There was nothing there.

Just an empty house.

"What's wrong?" Duncan asked again.

Cade ignored him, still searching. When he came to the end of the hallway he swore vehemently and turned back in Duncan's direction, scrambling to reach the stairway to the floor below.

As he passed, Duncan grabbed his arm, pulling him up short. "What's going on?"

"That was my wife!" Cade didn't even look at him as he replied, intent on reaching the lower floor and struggling to free himself.

Duncan did not understand and refused to relinquish his hold on his commander's arm. "What are you talking about?"

Cade spun around, fixing his subordinate in his baleful stare. "My wife. My wife was our guide. I need to find a way back to the Beyond, and I need to find it now!" He pulled free and rushed down the steps.

The stairs descended into a living room. It, too, was deserted and clearly unlived in for some time. Dust covered everything; the sofa, the matching armchairs, the glass-topped coffee table that stood between all three. The windows were bereft of curtain or blinds, and no pictures hung on the walls.

The living room was connected to a kitchen, and beyond that stood a formal dining room. Cade moved through them quickly, hoping that a three-bedroom home like this was would have more than one bath, as the mirror in the one upstairs had been missing, the discolored spot on the blue wallpaper the only evidence that one had once hung there at all.

A single door led off from the dining room and Cade made a beeline for it. The knob turned easily and he stepped inside.

It was, indeed, a second bathroom.

A toilet, a sink, and above that a mirror.

But as he stared at his distorted reflection in the few

remaining pieces of shattered glass that hung in the frame, Cade realized the futility of what he was doing. Even if the mirror had been whole, he wouldn't have been able to return to Gabbi. The Beyond just didn't work like that.

His frustration at being so close burned like a white-hot flame, threatening to consume him.

# CHAPTER 21

D UNCAN WATCHED CADE EMERGE FROM the rear of the house, trembling with barely concealed anger, and take a seat in one of the dust-covered chairs in the kitchen. He stared straight ahead at the wall in front of him, isolated by the weight of his emotion.

Choosing discretion over valor, Duncan kept his mouth shut, intent on giving his commanding officer time to cool off. Instead, he turned his attention to trying to figure out where they actually were and how they were going to get back to where they should be.

*All right, how hard can this be?* The first thing he tried was his cell phone, but either the battery was dead or the passage through to the Beyond had damaged it. There was a telephone mounted on the wall in the kitchen, but when he picked the receiver up, he found there was no dial tone. He'd expected as much, but it didn't hurt to be certain. Maybe an old newspaper or something with an address label on it? He rummaged around in the kitchen for several minutes, but came up empty. The drawers and the cabinets were bare. As were the corner tables in the living room.

*Perfect, just perfect.*

He returned to the kitchen to find Cade waiting for him.

"It's time to get some answers," was all the other man said, before leading Duncan through the house and out the front door into the cold night air without even a backward glance.

They found themselves at the very end of a long dirt road. On either side stretched barren fields as far as they could see.

There was nothing to do but start walking.

The temperature was above freezing, though not by much, Duncan figured. The sky above was clear, the stars shining brightly, and Duncan said a little prayer that it would stay that way.

They headed north, the only direction the road would take them. The bright moonlight illuminated their way perfectly.

Under other circumstances, it might have been an enjoyable stroll.

But for Duncan, it was anything but.

The last few days had opened his eyes wide with all that he'd seen and done. In just seventy-two hours, he'd been attacked by packs of revenants and flesh-hungry spectres, fought off a giant demon, journeyed to some other dimension under the power of a man known to most as the Heretic, and finally been rescued by his superior's wife, a woman who'd been dead for several years.

He had expected his time with Echo Team to be different than his work on the protective detail, but this was bordering on the absurd, particularly since he was now wandering in the middle of nowhere, trying to figure out just where in Creation they actually were.

They covered several miles, all in silence. The landscape did not change; they were surrounded by wide stretches of barren fields the entire distance.

About an hour after they started out, they came to a crossroads.

Ahead of them, the road continued onward, disappearing in a straight line into the darkness ahead.

To their right, it did the same.

To their left, however, it continued for several hundred yards before reaching the edge of a dark wood. There, it curved around the trees and out of sight.

Cade stood in the middle of the road and tried the radio phone again, but still no luck. He replaced it in his pocket, looked at Duncan, and shrugged. "Take your pick," he said.

The younger man pointed to the left. "At the very least, we'll be able to look at something other than these darn fields."

They set off again, this time walking side by side. They reached the tree line and followed the road as it curved to the left.

There, just around the corner, was a gas station.

The pumps were gone; the caps in the raised concrete dividers the only evidence they'd even existed. The large neon sign that had once stood proudly over the facility was reduced now to a single G, dark and lonely on its pedestal. The exterior walls of the station were covered with graffiti and a thick sheen of dust covered the windows, but it couldn't have been mistaken for anything but an old gas station.

Beneath the streetlight in the corner stood a battered old Coke machine, its front smashed open. Next to it, under the single streetlamp that lit the scene, was a pay phone.

With Cade following behind him, Duncan jogged over to the phone and picked up the receiver.

It came free in his hand, the severed end of the cord hanging free.

"Damn!" he said, throwing it aside.

He turned away from the phone and moved over to the station itself. Rubbing his sleeve against a window, Duncan cleared a section of dirt and grime as best he could, then peered inside. He could just make out several empty sets of shelves, a smashed refrigerator case, and a cashier's station.

Behind the counter, faded and torn but still tacked firmly to the wall, was a large map.

The front door was unlocked, long since having fallen victim to a few well-placed kicks. Duncan climbed over the counter to look at the map.

In the dim light coming in from outside, he could see that it was a large scale map of northern New York, so at least they were still in the same state.

But if the big red "You Are Here" symbol was correct, the deserted gas station he now stood in was more than fifty miles away from where they started.

It was going to be a long walk back.

\* \* \*

As the search for Duncan and Cade continued, Riley and Olsen turned their attention to trying to determine the significance of the information they'd been entrusted with. They borrowed several squads of men from Major Barnes and began checking out the most likely possibilities. Maps and GPS coordinates were cross-checked. Teams were dispatched to the nearest public libraries, searching their catalogs for books with a catalog number that might match. Train stations, bus stations, airports, health clubs, all were searched for a locker with the proper number and combination. State driver's license records were clandestinely searched, hoping for a match.

Several hours after the search got under way, they had their answer.

Fifteen miles from Stone's residence, a locker bearing the designation B27 was located. The remaining numbers proved to be the combination that opened it. Inside, the search team found a sealed packet of files. The information was collected and brought back to the Broadmoor commandery, where it was turned over to Sergeant Riley.

He and Olsen wasted no time in going through it. It contained daily logs and activity reports from the *Custodes Veritatis* going back several months, in which Commander Stone made more than one reference to his belief that there was a mole within his unit. He'd been unable to pinpoint a source, though, and had been left only with circumstantial evidence and no real suspect to tie to it. Included with the packet was another file, this time centering on a man named Simon Logan, a self-proclaimed mystic, who had expressed a sudden interest in the mystical Spear of Longinus. The evidence Stone had collected was slim, and several years out-of-date, but one particular detail caught their attention. In the margins of one of his reports, Stone had drawn the number nine surrounded by a snake eating its own tail. Beneath it, he'd written "Council of Nine?"

At last, the Enemy had a name.

* * *

Late that evening their missing comrades finally made contact from the pay phone in the lobby of a Days Inn some 75 miles away. A car was sent for them, and Echo's command team was reunited just as the sun was clearing the horizon.

Each group filled the other in on what had happened in their absence; Cade and Duncan describing their battle with the sorcerers and their subsequent escape to the Beyond, Riley and Olsen outlining the assistance they'd received in the search for Cade and the file they'd located at the bus station.

It was readily apparent to all of them that the Preceptor knew more than he'd revealed. After weighing his options, Cade decided it was time to pay the man a visit.

# CHAPTER 22

P RECEPTOR MICHAELS HAD JUST FINISHED his
morning cup of coffee when the door to his office
burst open and his personal aide, Donaldson, was
tossed inside to land in a heap on the carpet in front of his desk.

Behind him, the Heretic stalked into the room, the anger
evident on his face. With him was the Preceptor's former
security chief, Sean Duncan. Through the open doorway
Michaels could see Cade's two other sergeants, Riley and Olsen,
taking up guard positions outside the door.

"You lied to me," Cade said flatly.

"And a good morning to you too, Commander," Michaels
replied, outwardly maintaining his casual air while his mind
worked to figure out the angles. Donaldson, a thin man with a
narrow face, scrambled to his feet, still protesting the intrusion
and doing his best to explain to the Preceptor how he had tried to
keep the men out of the office. Michaels waved his hand,
indicating to the frantic man that everything was all right. "Fine,
fine, Donaldson, yes, thank you for your help. Now please
excuse us while the Commander and I have a chat."

Cade waited until the other man had left the room before speaking again. This time his voice took on a decidedly menacing air. "You put my people in unnecessary danger for political expediency. Tell me why I shouldn't just put a bullet through your skull to keep it from happening again."

Michaels stood, facing the Echo Team leader squarely. "I did no such thing, Commander. And if you ever threaten me again, I'll have you locked up faster than you can blink."

Duncan spoke up. "You need to listen to him, sir." While he said it respectfully, it was clearly not a request.

The Preceptor looked at him briefly, then turned his attention back to the Heretic. "If you'll curb that notorious temper of yours, I'm quite certain we can get to the bottom of whatever is bothering you." To quell some of the tension in the room, he came out from behind his desk and moved over to the wheeled breakfast cart standing in one corner. He poured himself a cup of coffee and offered the same to the other two men.

Cade snorted. "I don't have time for social niceties and other bullshit. Get to the point."

Michaels let some steel creep into his own tone. "I'm getting to the point, *Commander.*" He took a sip of his coffee, added more sugar. Still standing, he asked, "Just why do you believe I lied to you?"

The anger was still clear in Cade's voice. "You set us up without telling us the details." Cade mimicked the Preceptor's voice, "I need a combat team on this one; an investigative unit just won't do." His voice rose. "Of course you did. More specifically, you needed *my* combat team; who else would be crazy enough to take on the Adversary without help? You sent us in blind, and it's pure luck that all of my men are still standing at this point."

The Preceptor had visibly paled. "The Adversary? What are you talking about?"

"Don't play coy with me, Michaels. You've known all along whom that damned Necromancer was working for. Just as you've known what they were after. Did you think the existence of the *Custodes Veritatis* was a minor issue, nothing of any real importance to us? Did you truly believe we wouldn't find out about it?"

But Michaels wasn't playing coy. "You are correct. I chose not to disclose the existence of the Guardians to you. I see now that I should have, but as they say, hindsight is twenty-twenty. We operate on a need-to-know basis for very obvious reasons." The Preceptor attempted a smile, hoping to ease the mistrust that had developed between them. "You of all people should understand the need for operational security. But what does all this have to do with your Adversary?"

Cade's anger was partially an act, designed to get the Preceptor to make a mistake and reveal himself if he was a traitor. Appearing to look somewhat mollified, Cade gave out another tidbit as bait. "The sorcerers we've encountered have far more power than any currently active group we know of. They didn't just pick that knowledge up off the street; it takes years of practice and a direct connection to the demonic. In this case, their connection was the Adversary. The sorcerer leading the assault against the Broadmoor commandery had its particular stench all over him."

"That makes no sense, Commander. Based on your report this group doesn't number more than a handful of individuals. That's like jabbing a hornet's nest with a sharp stick."

Ignoring the Preceptor's question for the moment, Cade asked one of his own. "Operational security's a poor excuse if you knew the real targets of these attacks were the Guardians themselves."

"But we didn't know that. We still don't. And my oath to the Order prevented me from disclosing their existence or information about the relics they are supposed to protect. Now, however, I would say that it is time for you and Nigel Stone, the Guardians' commanding officer, to meet." The Preceptor reached for the phone.

Cade delivered his knockout punch, waiting the other man closely as he did.

"Stone's dead."

"What?" The phone dropped back into its cradle, and there was genuine shock on the Preceptor's face.

"Stone's dead. We found his gutted body in a safe house in upstate New York more than fifteen hours ago. From what we could tell, he'd been tortured extensively."

"Good Lord!" The Preceptor collapsed back into his chair, clearly unsettled by the news.

Cade went on, ruthlessly. "If we'd known earlier, if you'd told us everything we needed to know, we might have been able to save him. *He didn't have to die!*" He slammed his fist on the desk in frustration, then took a moment to regain control of his emotions. When he resumed speaking, his voice was level once again. "He was concerned about a leak in the Order. Did you know that?"

Still dazed by the news, the Preceptor nodded almost absently. "I've suspected it for some time, though I've been unable to pinpoint the source. Nigel was aware of my concerns. In fact, he was the one who convinced me of the problem."

"Great. Just what we need, a mole. As if a group of necromancers allied with the Adversary wasn't enough."

The Preceptor shook off his sorrow and focused on the discussion. "What do we know about the sorcerers?"

Cade stalked away from the desk and began to pace. "Stone left some information indicating he thought it was a small group known as the Council of Nine. While I wouldn't have put them at the top of the list on my own, everything we've uncovered so far ties neatly with the information Stone left for us. The group's leader, Simon Logan, has been a fringe player for some years, but has never shown this level of ability before."

"Another reason to believe they're getting outside help," said Duncan.

"But for what? What do they want? Are they crazy enough to think they can take on the entire Order?"

Cade shook his head. "They're not after the Order. They're after the Spear of Longinus." He outlined his conversation with the shade of Julius Spencer and used the visions he'd experienced in the Templeton cemetery as corroborating evidence. "If I'm going to be effective against our enemies, I'm going to have to know more about where and how the Spear is being stored," he said to the Preceptor.

Surprisingly, Michaels agreed. "I'll do better than that, Commander. I'll show it to you myself."

* * *

Like many of the other commanderies across the country, the one in Bristol extended below ground for several levels. It was there that much of the community's actual work took place; monitoring world events, training Templars on the latest high-tech weaponry, and the like. Here, hidden from view, lay the true work of the Order. The underground levels contained classrooms, laboratories, gymnasium facilities, a shooting range, and even a full-scale replica of a two-bedroom house used for live-fire exercises was tucked away in a large cavern on the third level below the surface.

Duncan and Cade were about to find out that below that level there was another, one that neither man had been aware of. It was the home of the *Custodes Veritatis*, the Guardians of Truth.

As they walked, the Preceptor brought the two men up to date.

"The Guardians have been in existence since just after World War II. Operating completely independently from the Order's normal chain of command, they have been charged with one purpose - protecting the Order's Holy Relics at all cost.

"At any given time there are only fifty active members. They are selected as much for their ability to deal with the extra natural as they are for their physical capabilities. The majority of them also have extremely high reserves of personal faith. About 20 percent of them have been ordained."

They went down several levels to where a long corridor stretched out before them. As they continued walking, Duncan asked, "Are they all stationed here?"

"No, though the majority are simply because this is where the Reliquary happens to be located at the moment. We move its location every few years, just to be on the safe side.

"The commander of the unit is always a senior officer known for his loyalty to the Order and his devout belief in the Lord. He reports to the North American Preceptor exclusively. Stone had been in command for the last ten years and was probably one of the best, if not *the* best, ever to have held the post."

A set of offices were on either side at the end of the hall; their interiors dark, their doors locked. Peering through a window,

Cade noted a standard office setup, complete with a calendar showing that day's date on the wall. All of them appeared perfectly normal, which Cade figured was precisely the intention. *Hide in plain sight*, he thought with respect to whoever had designed the place.

Reaching the end of the corridor, the Preceptor removed a chain from around his neck. On it were a standard metallic key and an electronic pass card. He inserted the key in the lock of the last office on the left, opened the door, and motioned for Cade and Duncan to follow. Without turning on the lights, he moved across the empty room to another door on the far side of the office. He held the pass card up to a small black box mounted next to the door. There was a soft beep, and the door opened inward.

Another corridor was revealed on the other side.

At the end, a guard station stood before a vault-like security door. There were two guards on duty, and one of them exchanged the daily password with the Preceptor, despite knowing him on sight. The Preceptor was then asked to place his hand in a small sensor unit mounted on the wall next to the door. A moment passed as the security device compared the digital image it held of his palm print to his actual hand. When the test was completed a chime sounded. Michaels stepped up in front of the door, stated his name in a clear voice, then followed that with a long series of numbers.

A few seconds after he finished speaking the door before him slid open without a sound.

"This way, gentlemen," he said.

On the other side of the door was a command center. Computerized monitoring stations were arrayed in a semicircle facing a large observation window, which in turn looked out over a room the size of a football field. Three men manned the workstations, and Cade could see several others moving about the floor of the room just beyond, where scores of items were sealed in special protective cases.

The Preceptor turned to them with a look of pride.

"Welcome to the Reliquary," he said.

# CHAPTER 23

"THIS IS INCREDIBLE," DUNCAN WHISPERED, and Cade had to agree.

It *was* incredible. On either side of them, vacuum-sealed chambers mounted on individual pedestals held artifacts both ancient and modern. From where he stood Cade could see Veronica's Veil, Moses' staff, a habit worn by Mother Teresa - the list went on. It was a veritable treasure house, even if only from a historical perspective. If just half of the things said about these items were true, then it was a collection that was absolutely priceless.

And full of power.

In the hands of the wrong people, people with the knowledge of how to harness that arcane power, many of these objects could cause widespread slaughter and destruction. It was no wonder the Order had locked them away for safekeeping.

Cade wandered among the rows for several more minutes, fascinated by what he saw. At last he turned to the Preceptor, a question on his lips.

"The Spear?"

The Preceptor smiled, anticipating the question.

"This way. It has a room of its own."

A side gallery was situated to the left of the main floor, and they found a watch captain on duty there. The captain had the Preceptor sign the logbook, then walked with him farther along the edge of the room until they came to a set of highly polished double doors. Here the Preceptor submitted to a retinal scan. When it was concluded, the system beeped once, and the doors opened.

As the doors slid open, the interior lights automatically came on, revealing a small room with a long, narrow, steel-reinforced glass display case in the center. The Preceptor held out a hand, indicating that they should enter.

Cade stepped forward. Inside the case, on a bed of white silk, was the head of a Roman lance. The blade itself was made of iron and was several inches in length, with a winged shape and an ornamental pin inserted down its center. Two additional wings had been added at the base and were tied to it with dark leather straps. The wood of the shaft looked new, and he assumed the original had long since been lost, but the blade had been remounted on a perfectly crafted length of polished oak some nine feet in length.

Peripherally, Cade saw Duncan genuflect, then sink to one knee in homage to the Spear.

Obviously his teammate was convinced of the Spear's authenticity, that this was indeed the very weapon that had pierced the side of the Messiah, but Cade himself was not so certain. He didn't have Duncan's faith and therefore didn't take the provenance of the weapon at face value. To test it further, he triggered his Sight.

Looked at through that perspective, the head of the lance was bathed in a brilliant golden glow, a glow so bright that Cade had to turn his face away to shield his eyes from its intensity.

Returning his vision to normal, Cade stepped away from the display case. Turning, he found the Preceptor watching him closely.

"Reach out your hand and put it in my side. Stop doubting, and believe," the older man said softly.

Cade didn't need to be a biblical scholar to recognize the passage regarding the Apostle Thomas, but he pretended he hadn't heard it. He wasn't about to argue faith with a man who hadn't walked the paths he'd walked, hadn't seen the things he'd seen. The thought of a weapon with that kind of power in the hands of the Necromancer made his skin crawl. To have it fall into the hands of the Adversary was unthinkable.

Duncan finally arose, his impromptu prayers done, and rejoined them by the door. "What now?" he asked.

Cade caught the Preceptor's eye. "In the end, Stone probably told them what they wanted to know, you realize."

The Preceptor nodded. "Which means they'll be coming for the Spear."

"And anything else they can get their hands on," Cade replied.

"So do we move it now, while we have the chance?" Duncan wanted to know.

Cade shook his head. "While the final decision is up to the Preceptor, I'd say no. We have adequate defenses here, and we know what we are up against. Moving the Spear simply puts us at a disadvantage. If there is a mole, and he were to leak the information, we'd be on unfamiliar ground, with only a small force to protect the weapon in the event of an attack. Staying here means we know the territory, can better anticipate and, therefore, prevent any action the Enemy might take."

"I agree," said the Preceptor. "How do you suggest we prepare the defenses?"

Cade gave it some thought. "Based on the attack in New York, we know they are conjuring up darker forces and using them to breach the gates. I'd expect them to do the same again; without knowing we're on to them, they'll continue using the same strategy they've employed in that past." As he spoke, Cade headed back toward the control room, the other two men half a step behind. "We'll need to be ready to deal with the supernatural side of their forces. First we get the troops we have on immediate alert. For all we know, the Council could strike at any moment, so we want to be protected to some degree in case they do. In the meantime I would suggest activating the rest of Echo Team and possibly Bravo as well. Once they get here, we should have enough men to hold the commandery indefinitely, provided we can neutralize their sorcery early in the game. We also need to get our own mystics into position ASAP. Have them raise the wards around the property, make it as difficult as possible for the Council to enter the grounds."

"Very good. I'll turn defense of the complex over to you, Knight Commander," said Michaels. "I'll take active control of the *Veritatis* soldiers and coordinate the defense of the Reliquary with you as we move forward."

The defense of the Spear had begun.

# CHAPTER 24

HOURS PASSED, AND THERE WAS still no sign of the enemy. Daylight gave way to night. During the day Cade made regular visits along the defenses, to see that the men were ready.

Still, the Enemy did not come.

Frustrated by the long wait, Cade decided to take a walk. He hoped the exercise would clear the haze from his thoughts, refocus his attention on the matter at hand. Without any clear destination in mind, he reentered the house and began to make his way through the halls, lost in thought.

A short time later he found himself in a quiet corridor somewhere in the depths of the lower levels. Around him, all was silent. Ahead of him, a soft light spilled forth from an open door at the end of the hallway.

The light beckoned.

Curious, Cade moved to investigate.

As he got closer, he could see that the door opened onto a small chapel.

It was a simple affair; several rows of wooden pews standing before an altar. A large wooden crucifix hung on the wall above. Off to the left, in a small alcove all its own, was a statue of the Blessed Virgin Mother hemmed in by scores of votive candles. It was their light that had captured Cade's attention.

He paused in the doorway, considering.

It had been a long time since he'd spoken to God, longer still since he'd set foot in a place of worship. It was a situation he rarely considered consciously, though the irony of the truth of it in conjunction with his nickname among the rest of the Order was not lost on him. But there he stood in the doorway, too tired even to think up an excuse for turning away.

So instead, he stepped inside.

He walked between the rows of pews, running his hand along their polished wood surface. He skirted the altar, refusing to look up at the face on the cross, and moved to stand in front of the statue of the Virgin. Her gentle face looked down upon him, her expression frozen forever in compassion and pain, hope and loss. The light of the votive candles at her feet reflected off her smooth alabaster skin, softening the hard angles and cold stone.

Looking down, Cade noted that one candle in the center of the group remained unlit.

On impulse, he picked up the taper lying nearby and lit the candle.

"For you, Gabbi. A light to guide you home."

His voice sounded overly loud in the quiet of the room.

His pain was echoed in that emptiness.

The statue gazed down at him in sympathy and kindness but without any answers to the depths of his loss.

Moving away from the alcove, he took a seat in one of the pews facing the altar, feeling out of place, a stranger in a strange land. Once, long ago, he'd believed in the divine grace of God, of his intended plan for the salvation of his people. He'd been a faithful churchgoer, finding comfort in the Sunday ceremonies, a balm for the chaos he faced each day on the force.

All of that had been shattered on a summer night seven years ago.

For the first time since entering the room, Cade allowed his gaze to rest on the figure nailed to the crucifix above the altar. Accusations and anger filled his heart as he stared at the face of the one known as the Lamb of God.

*Lamb is right*, Cade thought. *Off to the slaughter you went, without even a hand raised in resistance. Where, then, was the Lion of Judah? Where was the one who ordered the demons to flee, the one who faced the darkness of the Evil One?*

*I'll tell you where.*

*Abandoned by your Father and left to die.*

*Just as my Gabrielle was abandoned in her hour of need.*

Cade looked away. He'd lost his faith at the moment he'd lost her. Nothing since had managed to heal that wound. The events of the last few days had started it bleeding anew.

Had it really been her? He struggled to come up with a definitive answer. His mind said yes; he'd heard her voice, seen her face, felt the love for him that flowed from her like a gentle caress. Yet his heart said no. It couldn't be her. Believing it meant that instead of finding that promised salvation in the heaven she'd always believed in, she was left to roam that horrid wasteland on the other side of the barrier. A hundred different questions drifted through his mind. How long had she been there? What had happened to her since the night she'd been taken from his side? Why had it taken her so long to reveal herself to him? Had he done something to damn her for all eternity?

And the biggest one of all.

What caring God would send her there in the first place?

He raised his face to the cross once more. *You left us when we needed you most. Is it any wonder that I turned my back on You in return?*

The man hanging on the cross had no answer.

Cade had not expected one.

He'd long gotten used to working on his own.

A glance at his watch told him he'd been in the chapel for half an hour. Knowing he'd be useless unless he managed to get some rest, Cade got up and walked out, headed to his quarters, never once looking back.

Behind him, in the empty chapel, the candles were slowly snuffed out one by one as if by an unseen hand.

Only the candle Cade himself had started was left to burn, its solitary light shining steadfastly against the darkness that swept in to surround it.

\* \* \*

Cade awoke.

It was not the slow, gentle awakening he had known in his earlier years before the harsh realities of life had became commonplace. Nor was it the swift rise to alertness that had characterized his time as a STOP team leader. This was electrifying, brutal in its suddenness, like being dropped into icy cold water. It caused his heart to drum in his chest and his breath to come in short, sharp gasps.

Wide-eyed, he stared for a moment at the nearest wall, his senses on high alert. He was overcome with the unmistakable feeling that there was someone in the room with him, close, very close; the hair on his back was standing stiffly upright as if charged by a massive amount of static electricity.

Yet his danger sense had not kicked in. He did not feel the need to reach for his gun or get out of the way of an impending blow; in fact, what he felt was more a rising sense of curiosity than anything else.

Slowly, ever so slowly, he rolled over.

Even in the dim lighting he could clearly see the woman who was standing in his doorway only a few feet away.

Gabrielle.

"Hello, Cade," she said, softly.

She wore the same robe she'd worn in the Beyond, the hood pulled up to partially obscure her face, but Cade knew without a doubt that it was truly her.

He scrambled to his feet. "Gabbi? Gabbi!" he exclaimed, rushing closer, his arms outstretched as if to hold her.

"No!" she shouted, stepping back, one hand upraised to stop him. "Don't touch me!"

Cade pulled up short, only steps away, pain and confusion chasing each other across his face.

In response, she reached up and withdrew her hood, revealing her face. Her soft skin, her rich full lips, the elegant curve of her throat – Cade could only stare in stunned amazement.

But before he could ask how the transformation had occurred, Gabrielle's face began to shift. Like a mirage wavering in the heat, the phantom mask behind which she had hidden herself faded away.

Cade was left staring at the same sight he had seen on that summer night seven years ago, her face stripped of its skin, her beautiful eyes staring out at him through a sea of bloodied flesh.

The mask returned as swiftly as it had faded, but the point

had been made.

Without a word, she pointed to his hands.

Cade glanced down at his bare skin and suddenly understood.

He'd removed his gloves when he'd lain down to sleep. With his hands bare, his Gift was ready for use whether he wanted it or not. Gabrielle, in turn, appeared as solid as she had in life. This was no ghost or shade, intruding where it didn't belong, but his wife, brought back and seemingly whole again. Touching her would have been like touching one of the living, he would have been bombarded with her thoughts, emotions, and memories.

Gabrielle took a step closer to him. "You must hurry, my love. While you wait, the Enemy has already breached your defenses. They're inside the walls, getting closer every minute to what they came for."

"What?" Cade replied, confused. He couldn't seem to focus, his emotions flaring like a storm-swept sea; his soul ached at the knowledge of her loss, while his heart shouted with joy to see her standing before him.

Her voice grew stern. "There's no time. You must get to the Reliquary. You must protect the Spear!"

"How did you get here? Where have you been? What's happened to you, Gabbi?" Cade was suddenly frantic with a need for information. He had to know that he had not failed her.

But Gabrielle would have none of it. "Listen to me!" she cried, startling Cade into silence. "You've got to act, before it's too late. Hurry! If the Spear falls into his hands, all will be lost. Go, go!"

With her final shout still ringing in the air, Gabrielle vanished.

# CHAPTER 25

ADE HEADED FOR THE RELIQUARY at a dead run. On his way he used his radio to raise the alarm, so that by the time he reached the entrance to the lower levels he found Riley and Olsen waiting for him, weapons in hand. Duncan appeared out of an adjoining corridor seconds later.

Cade wasted no time with long explanations. "We're under attack, and I suspect our defenses have already been breached. Olsen, get us some backup. We'll meet you in the Reliquary, unless we run into serious resistance before we get there." Nodding at Riley and Duncan, he said, "You two are with me. Watch your backs."

As Olsen disappeared back the way he had come, the other three cautiously descended the stairs leading to the hidden corridor Michaels had revealed to them earlier that morning.

They moved forward quickly, knowing that every moment might be the difference between success and failure, between saving a life and ending one. They passed through the outer rooms, and then through the final tunnel that led to the

Reliquary.

It was there that they received their first confirmation of what Gabbi had foretold. Both guards were missing from their stations, and the reinforced vault door to the Reliquary was standing wide open.

The sound of Cade chambering a round into his weapon was surprisingly loud in the still tunnel.

"Keep your eyes open," he said, moving through the door with the other two at his heels.

The scene that met their eyes was incomprehensible.

*Earthquake.* That was Cade's initial thought. And, indeed, it was easy to imagine that an earthquake had occurred, considering the devastation before them.

But Cade knew the answer wouldn't prove that benign.

The monitoring room was a disaster. Computerized monitoring stations lay strewn across the floor. So, too, did the filing cabinets and desk drawers. Looking through the viewing window they could see that the Reliquary chamber itself had been ransacked. One section of the room seemed to have been consumed in a great fire. Scorch marks covered the walls, floor, and even the ceiling. The fire response system must have gone off, for water still rained down throughout the room, and puddles pooled here and there on the floor. The glass chambers that had once housed the precious artifacts had been destroyed where they stood, the glass shattered across the floor and pedestals. The relics themselves were either missing, destroyed, or buried among the rubble. The great steel doors that had led to the secondary vault where the Spear itself had been stored had been torn off their hinges and lay haphazardly against other debris. Oddly, their smooth, polished surfaces seemed unsullied by the dust and soot that coated most of the rest of the room.

Cade and his men quickly moved inside.

The side gallery where the watch commander's office had been was gone completely, buried under a mound of fallen earth, concrete, and steel.

Similar piles of debris were scattered throughout the room.

Cade stood at the center of the disaster, amazed at the destruction.

*How in God's name did they do this? Why didn't we hear anything up above?* It seemed impossible that they could have accomplished so much in so short a time.

Another question loomed.

*How did they get in?*

"Commander."

The voice was little more than a whisper, but it was enough. Cade bent down, peered into the pile of debris in front of him, and began digging through it furiously. Duncan and Riley jumped in to lend a hand. Olsen showed up seconds later with several other Templars, men Duncan recognized as members of the Preceptor's security detail. They fanned out and began to search the place in more detail. Soon the badly wounded bodies of Preceptor Michaels and his aide, Jonathan Donaldson, were pulled free from the rubble. A medical team was sent for immediately.

Donaldson was drifting in and out of consciousness, but didn't appear to be mortally wounded. Michaels, however, was clearly in trouble. A wide gash split his forehead from just above his eye all the way back past his right ear. His left arm was bent at a strange angle below the elbow, and a wide bloodstain spread across the front of his shirt.

Duncan and Cade carried him over to clear a spot on the floor and set him down gently. As Duncan tried to staunch the thin stream of blood from the Preceptor's head wound, Cade tore open the man's shirt to get a look at his injuries.

A large gaping wound could be seen just below the left side of the man's ribcage, the occasional flash of glistening pink revealing the damage to internal organs. Minor knife cuts and what appeared to be bite wounds covered his chest, arms, and legs. To make matters worse, the Preceptor was still losing blood at a tremendous rate as his heart fought to keep it pumping through his damaged form.

"Can you do anything for him?" Cade asked.

"As soon as the medics get here, we can . . ."

"That's not what I'm talking about and you know it. We don't have time to wait for the medics. He'll be dead by then!"

Duncan looked up defiantly. "Then no. No, I can't do anything for him." He'd vowed not to use his strange power. It was a vow he intended to keep, no matter what the circumstances.

Cade had other ideas, though. His hand moved to the gun at his side. "I'm giving you an order, Sergeant. I don't care what your personal problems might be; you're going to do what you can to save this man."

The muzzle of the gun inched upward slightly.

The two men stared at each other.

* * *

In the end, it wasn't the threat of the gun that caused Duncan to give in. He'd spent the last three years protecting this man day and night. He had the power to save him now. *How could he not use it?*

Duncan gently lowered Michaels's head to the floor and

moved to the Preceptor's side. "I'll give it a try. He's lost a lot of blood."

"Do what you can."

Duncan placed his hands on either side of the bloody gap in the injured man's flesh. Bowing his head, he closed his eyes and called upon his power.

To everyone else it looked like Duncan was simply praying over the older man, but thanks to his Sight, Cade could see the brilliant blue glow that suddenly burst from Duncan's palms, bathing Michaels in its light. As Cade watched the outer edges of the wound began to knit together, flesh merging with flesh. The flow of blood slowed, but did not stop.

Suddenly the light flared, spluttered, and died.

Cade glanced anxiously at his teammate. "What happened?"

"I'm . . . not sure."

Duncan's hair was disheveled and rivers of sweat streamed down his face from the effort. He shook his head as if to clear it, shifted his hands slightly, and tried again. This time, the light merely flickered once before dying out. Duncan kept at it for several more minutes, to no avail.

Finally, he slumped back on his heels, exhausted and confused. "I've never encountered anything like this before. It's as if something is actively working to resist my efforts."

Despite all he had done, blood was still flowing from the chest wound. And there was very little else they could do for Michaels.

Michaels must have understood his situation, for he suddenly tried to speak to them. Whatever he meant to say, however, was drowned in a fit of coughing.

"Easy, Preceptor, easy. Help is on the way," Duncan told him, holding his hand for reassurance.

But the Preceptor would not be silenced. He tried again, but couldn't get the words out around the sudden stream of blood that surged up out of his throat. His message dissolved into a fit of hacking as he sought to clear his airway and to draw another breath into his punctured lungs.

Cade knew that the man had only moments left to live. Without Duncan's attempt at healing, he wouldn't have survived even this long. Whatever he was trying to tell them was about to be lost forever.

Knowing he had no other choice, Cade made a decision. Stripping off his right glove, he seized Michaels's bare hand in his own.

*Darkness.*

*Chaos.*

*Figures rushing about; the stench of decay heavy in the air; shouts of pain, of fear. He turns, determined to raise the alarm, to let the others know that the attack is under way.*

*A figure is suddenly there before him, blocking the way to the exit.*

*He pauses, and that is his mistake. A moment of chilling cold as something shoves its way into his flesh, then pain, terrible pain, the kind of pain that drowns out everything else in a great overwhelming curtain of white noise, cutting, tearing, savage pain.*

*A hand grasps the back of his neck, pulling him closer, driving whatever it is farther into his body, twisting, turning, the pain echoing, building, reverberating through his very soul.*

*Hot breath in his ear, a familiar voice, "Die, you bastard!"*

*Then falling, falling, the impact with the floor barely felt as the pain reaches up and engulfs him in its tender arms, nestling him in its horrifying embrace.*

*As darkness threatens, a face looms before him.*

*A familiar face.*

*And then the voice again, a whispered, "Rot in hell, Fool."*

Cade jerked his hand free, stopping the flow of images.

Duncan opened his mouth to ask what Cade had seen, but the expression of rage on the commander's face caused him to swallow his question unasked. He watched in amazement as Cade surged to his feet and stalked across the room to where the Preceptor's aide, Donaldson, was being tended by two of the other soldiers. Pushing them aside, Cade reached down, seized the injured man by his lapels, and hauled him to his feet.

"You son of a bitch!" Cade screamed at the other man, shaking him as he did. "Where are they?"

Several of the other Knights rushed forward, intent on helping Donaldson, but Riley and Olsen swiftly interposed themselves between the injured man and his would-be rescuers, protecting their superior with guns drawn.

Duncan could only kneel there, stunned, the tension in the room going from bad to worse as the men from the protective detail drew their own weapons in response.

The room dissolved into chaos. Cade was yelling questions at Donaldson, who though obviously terrified, refused to answer. The local Knights were trying to edge closer in an attempt to pull the two men apart, while Cade's men worked to keep them at bay. Threats and commands were flying left and right, no one listening to either.

Finally, Duncan had had enough. He drew his pistol, pointed it across the room at a pile of debris, and pulled the trigger.

The echoing gunshot brought everyone, including Cade, up short.

Into the silence, Duncan said, "Preceptor Michaels is dead."

For a long moment, no one moved or spoke. Then, "And this piece of shit is the reason," replied Cade. He tossed Donaldson to the floor in disgust and anger. "He lowered the wards and let the Enemy in through some kind of back door. When Michaels discovered his treachery, Donaldson killed him."

"How can you know that?" asked one of the locals.

"Because the Preceptor told him," Duncan replied quickly, cutting Cade off before he could answer himself. The last thing they needed at that moment was a discussion of the Heretic's powers. He would deal with the Commander's wrath later; right now they needed to defuse the situation. The men from the detail knew him. They'd be far more prone to believe a simple explanation from him than one from Williams.

\* \* \*

Cade stood back and watched as Duncan marched over to Donaldson and began questioning him under the watchful eyes of the locals.

"You okay, boss?"

Cade turned to find Riley at his elbow, watching him.

"Yeah," he said, spitting the taste of dust and debris out of his mouth. "That son of a bitch did this. He knows where that bastard Logan is. He might even know how to find the Adversary. He's going to tell us what he knows. And I intend to make him pay for what he's done here."

But it didn't look like Duncan was getting anywhere. His questions were met with silence. Donaldson stared at the floor, ignoring everything that was said to him. From where he stood Cade could hear his teammate's voice raised in anger at the prisoner's indifference, but he knew that without any real threat, the traitor would simply keep his mouth shut. The longer he did so, the farther away his accomplices could get with the stolen relics and the less chance the Templars would have in recovering the Spear.

Something needed to be done, and it needed to be done quickly.

Cade glanced around, taking in the positions of the men in the room. His gaze fell upon the doors that had once guarded the entrance to the secondary vault.

Duncan stepped over to his teammates. "We're not getting anywhere. We're going to take him upstairs to one of the interview rooms and let him stew for a while. Then we'll take another shot at him. Don't worry, we'll get what we need out of him."

Cade ignored the statement. He'd already decided on another course of action, and it didn't involve further delay. He remained standing between Olsen and Riley, waiting for his chance.

Duncan took charge of the Knights, ordering two of them to get Donaldson on his feet and the others to begin searching the room for any other bodies or missing artifacts that might be uncovered.

With Duncan in the lead, the small group made its way toward the exit.

"The hell with this," Cade said beneath his breath.

He waited until the group had come abreast of him, then made his move. He stepped between his men, reached out, and grabbed Donaldson. He pulled him close, one arm around the man's neck, the other holding the barrel of his pistol to Donaldson's head.

Everyone, including Riley and Olsen, were taken by surprise. They stepped toward him, but Cade had wasted as much time as he intended, and he let them know it.

"Don't even think about it," he said, twisting the barrel of his gun sharply against the prisoner's skull. "I'll put a bullet through his brain faster than you think. I don't need him alive to discover what he knows."

It was a bluff, pure and simple, designed to let his men know that he hadn't completely lost it, at the same time using his reputation to keep the other Knights at bay.

It worked, for the group froze where they stood, waiting to see what he would do.

Cade had timed his move perfectly and stood with his back to the pile of debris on which the steel doors that once guarded the entrance to the secondary vault now rested.

He needed time to question Donaldson properly, needed the freedom to do it his way. He didn't stop to think, didn't stop to analyze the possible success or failure of what he intended to do. Instead, he simply threw himself backward at the reflective surface of the doors without letting go of the stranglehold on Donaldson.

As the rest of the soldiers in the room watched in shocked surprise, Cade and his unwilling passenger struck the reflective surface of the doors and disappeared into the Beyond.

# CHAPTER 26

T HE SUN WAS JUST RISING over the treetops when Cade appeared at the gate outside the commandery. Word of what had happened in the Reliquary must have spread, for he noted that the guards opened the gate and waved him through without a word. He noted the fear in their eyes as he passed. One soldier even crossed himself when he thought the other man wasn't looking.

And with that the legend of the Heretic grew.

*So be it*, he thought. He was under too much pressure at the moment to care. He'd deal with the fallout later.

Cade had one of the guards transport him down the long drive and to the manor house. Once inside he went immediately to the Preceptor's office. Two guards stood outside, but they made no move to stop him as he stepped up to the doors, found them unlocked, and disappeared inside the office.

After that it only took him a few more moments to get the video-conferencing equipment powered up. Placing the call, he stood in front of the screen, waiting for the connection to be made.

The call went through quickly. Cade wasn't surprised to find that someone had been specifically detailed to wait for any incoming messages. The higher-ups would want to know as much as possible as soon as possible.

When Cardinal Giovanni finally appeared, however, it was clear that he was disappointed to see Cade.

"Knight Commander Williams," he said, with a bit of a frown as he took his seat before the camera. "Where, may I ask, is Preceptor Michaels?"

"I'm sorry to report that Preceptor Michaels is dead, Your Eminence."

Giovanni's expression remained steady, though Cade thought he saw his lips tighten ever so slightly. "What happened?"

Cade explained how Michaels had died and what he had learned from his interrogation of Donaldson; how the traitor had disabled the wards and granted the Necromancer's troops access to the grounds, how he had led them into the manor house and down through the lower levels to the Reliquary itself, how he had fooled the Preceptor into opening the sanctuary to the very enemy he was trying to protect it from. He saved the worst for last.

"The Council probably has the Spear in its possession by now, Eminence. Logan more than likely also has a significant number of other artifacts along with it; the investigation team is still trying to determine what was destroyed versus what is missing from the Reliquary."

"I don't need to tell you how dangerous this situation has become, do I, Knight Commander?"

Cade shook his head. "No, Your Eminence, you don't. That's why I've taken the liberty of calling up both Echo and Bravo Teams and putting them on combat alert. Donaldson gave us the location of the Council's stronghold in Louisiana. I intend to stage a combined air and land assault against it before nightfall. All I need is your approval, sir." *I don't even truly need that*, he thought to himself, *but it doesn't hurt to play nice in the sandbox now and then.*

"Of course, Knight Commander. You have my permission to do whatever, I repeat, *whatever*, is necessary to recover the Spear."

"Thank you, sir."

As Cade reached for the disconnect button, the Cardinal leaned forward and asked another question. "What have you done with the traitor, Knight Commander?"

Without hesitation Cade answered, "I've got him secured in a place where he can't cause us any further harm."

Cardinal Giovanni nodded. "Good, good. When we've finished with the Necromancer and recovered the Spear, we'll want to see to it that justice is served."

For the first time in days, the Knight Commander smiled. "Have no fear, Your Eminence. Justice will be served. I'll take care of it personally."

\* \* \*

Olsen, Riley, and Duncan had just finished eating when Cade strode into the dining hall. The Knight Commander was still dressed in the same clothing he had worn the night before, bloodstains and all, and conversation among the other tables drifted to a stop as the rest of the men in the room got a good look at him. Cade barely noticed the effect he was having on those around him as he crossed to where Olsen was sitting and laid a piece of paper on the table before him. On it was the address in southern Louisiana that Donaldson had given to him.

"I need to know as much as possible about that location, and I need it in thirty minutes," Cade told him. Turning to Riley, he said, "That's how long you have to assemble the squad leaders from Echo and Bravo Teams and get them in the air with their men to the Lafayette commandery in Louisiana. We'll meet them there later this afternoon. We're running out of time, and I don't intend to waste another minute more."

Duncan got to his feet, a confused look on his face. "Where is Donaldson?" he asked, looking past the Knight Commander as if expecting him to enter the room behind him.

Cade ignored him, still concentrating on Riley.

"We're going after the Spear. I want the Blackhawk pilots on alert and the armorers ready to outfit the assault teams. Be certain you've . . ."

"What did you do with Donaldson?"

Duncan's voice was loud and cutting, his eyes full of anger.

Silence fell.

The two men stared at each other.

Olsen tried to intervene. "Duncan, I don't think now is . . ."

Duncan cut him off with a wave of his hand without taking his attention from Cade. "I asked you a question, *sir*. I want to know what happened to Donaldson."

Cade placed both fists on the table and leaned forward so that his face was inches from Duncan's own. Softly, he said, "I left him behind, where he belongs."

Duncan pulled back, the confusion on his face evident.

Cade watched as a look of horror slowly crossed the younger man's face, but the Commander was past caring. He'd spent the last three hours forcing the location of the Council's stronghold out of the traitor, hours that should have been spent going after the Spear. He no longer had the time to cater to the other man's precious sense of fair play.

The Necromancer and his allies had declared war.

Cade intended to give them one.

He turned away, believing the conversation to be finished, but Duncan's voice caused him to turn back again.

"You killed him." Duncan said, and his tone spoke volumes.

Cade stared directly into the younger man's eyes, speaking slowly and clearly so there could be no further misunderstandings.

"No, I left him in the Beyond."

With grim satisfaction, Cade remembered looking back from the edge of the portal to where Donaldson stood in the middle of a mist-encircled field in the Beyond. In the distance, the howling cries of the oncoming spectres that had picked up their scent could be heard, drowning out the man's pleas for mercy as Cade returned to the real world without him.

The Echo Team leader watched Duncan's eyes grow wider as the impact of his statement registered, and he couldn't resist a parting shot.

"Considering what was closing in on him, I'd say that killing him would have been a blessing. Which is precisely why I left him alive and well."

The room was absolutely silent as he turned on his heel and walked out.

* * *

Seven hours later the command elements for both Echo and Bravo Teams were assembled in a large conference room on the second floor of the training center at the Lafayette commandery in Louisiana. Riley, Olsen, and Duncan had been joined by the rest of Echo Team's squad leaders; Martinez, First Squad's fiery Latino; Wilson, Second Squad's temperamental preacher, Baker and Lyons, Third and Fourth Squads grizzled veterans. Also present were the four officers from Bravo Team; Swanson, Mace, Kurita, and Pantolano. The rest of the two teams' members were waiting in the main facility one floor below them.

Several free standing bulletin boards were set up in the front of the room. One contained a map of the state of Louisiana, with the target site circled in red southwest of where they presently were. Another contained old sepia photographs of a plantation house. Each of its two stories was surrounded by a wide veranda, with prominent columns. On the right side, the home was connected to what appeared to be a two-story greenhouse or conservatory. Separate photos showed additional buildings; a stable, a garage, others whose purposes were not immediately apparent.

A wider-angle photo on the next board showed how the lawn ran down to the water's edge, where a boathouse had been built next to a dock that extended out into the bayou itself.

Duncan paid close attention to the photos, memorizing as much of the detail as possible. In the heat of a major firefight things could get confusing very quickly and he didn't want to be at a disadvantage if he became separated from the main assault group.

*Provided the commander even keeps me in the unit*, he thought sourly, remembering his outburst from earlier that morning.

Duncan's concern was unnecessary, for Cade had already dismissed the incident from his mind. He had far more important issues to focus on.

"All right, listen up," Cade said loudly as he moved to the front of the room. He waited a moment for the chatter to quiet down, and then continued in a quieter tone. "As you know, several of our commanderies have been attacked this week. We've managed to identify the group behind the assaults, and it's my intention to carry the battle to them this time. Riley?"

A large picture appeared on the wall behind Cade as Riley switched on the projector at the back of the room. The picture was of a man in his mid-thirties, with dark hair and beard, dressed in shabby and ill-fitted clothes. Duncan thought he had the lean look of a man fallen on hard times, despite the fire in the man's eyes.

"This is Simon Logan, a self-styled necromancer and leader of a group that calls itself the Council of Nine. We don't know much about them, other than a few basics. They have always been fringe players, minor-league at best, without any real talent or ability. Given the number of genuine threats we face on a regular basis, worrying about the wannabes is usually counterproductive and so we ignored the Council in favor of bigger targets. As it turns out, that was a mistake."

Cade turned away from the screen to address his men directly. "During the last few months, Logan and his followers have increased their knowledge of the dark arts to levels we never imagined they'd be able to achieve. My personal belief is that they have had some outside help – they've moved ahead too quickly to have done so on their own – but we do not yet have any concrete, tangible proof to that effect.

"Logan hasn't been seen in public in almost three years, yet all indications suggest he's still alive and running the show. His core group of followers, the 'nine' from the group's name, are seen only slightly more often, though we don't have anything better than blurry photos of men in hooded robes in an undisclosed location. Personal information on them is practically non-existent. Next slide, please."

The image of Logan was replaced by a blurry image of the plantation house. It had been taken from a distance, probably from a boat out on the bayou, and this time was in color. The quality was poor, but even so the men could see that the structure had fallen into disrepair, and the bayou had long since begun its encroachment on the property.

"This is the plantation as it is today. Or so we think. No one has been allowed on the property for several years. The man who took the picture, a real-estate developer looking to make a big score, had just come back from a clandestine visit to the site three years ago when he was killed in a hit-and-run accident while getting out of his car to visit the local coffee shop. The photo was the only one that the police were able to develop from the camera that he'd left on the front seat of his car. Next."

A photo of the Spear of Destiny followed.

"This is the Spear of Destiny, also known as the Spear of Longinus It is the weapon used by the Roman soldier of the same name to pierce the side of Christ at the crucifixion. For hundreds of years, people have believed that the weapon was either in the hands of the Vatican, safely ensconced in one of the pilasters that form the framework of Michelangelo's Dome, or in a display case in the Hofberg Treasure House in Vienna."

Cade looked up at the image, then back down at the men assembled before him. "I suspect you've all heard the news by now. Until last night, the real Spear was under our control in a special vault. What you probably haven't heard is that we were betrayed from within. A man named Donaldson, the Preceptor's personal aide, was, in fact, a mole working for the Council. As a result, Preceptor Michaels lost his life, and the Spear, along with several other important relics, vanished into the night in the hands of Logan's followers. It's our job to bring them back.

"We believe that Logan's men have returned to their headquarters in northern Louisiana and that they are unaware that we are on to them. They will more than likely remain at that location, believing they are safe, at least for the time being. It is my intention to use that false sense of security to our advantage. By this time tomorrow, I expect that facility to be in the hands of our Order."

The room buzzed with righteous excitement as the squad leaders acknowledged the mission before them and the chance they were being given to strike back at those who had dared to attack the Order.

The men quieted down as Cade revealed a large-scale map of the local area. The plantation's position was prominently noted. "Echo Team will take ground transportation to here," he said, indicating a landing some miles away on the edge of the bayou. "A guide has been arranged to take us through the swamp so we can approach the plantation from the swamp. Bravo Team will be inbound in the Blackhawks by then." Cade turned to face the Bravo commanders. "I want the men off-loaded and the choppers back out of the way as quickly as possible, understood?"

There was an answering chorus of yes sirs.

"Echo will take the plantation house, Bravo the surrounding buildings. Once the Spear is secured, we'll get it out of there aboard one of the choppers, then destroy the rest of the vermin."

"Questions?"

Kurita was first. "What can we expect by way of resistance?"

"We're not entirely certain. The Council had nine key members. We know two are dead. What we don't know is how many followers might be there on the property with the rest. We do know they are capable of calling forth a variety of nether creatures. We've faced revenants, spectres, and one minor demon in the last three days alone; so be prepared for anything once we hit the ground. We're going to be going in fast and hard, with surprise on our side, but if we get bogged down in a long firefight, the odds will be on their side.

"Firepower?" Mace asked.

"Again, uncertain, though all of the Council members we've seen to date have eschewed weaponry in favor of their ritual magick."

Martinez raised his hand next. "What are the rules of engagement regarding prisoners?"

"I don't expect there to be any, as they're not the type to surrender. If by some strange chance they do, you've got to be extremely careful that it's not just a ploy to bring you within their reach. Cuffs, gags, and blindfolds, at a minimum, on every prisoner. You need to be absolutely certain that they cannot make use of their arcane abilities."

"Understood."

"We'll have one chance at this, gentlemen. Once they know we're on to them, they disappear like rats into the woodwork. The Spear is too dangerous to leave in their hands. We cannot allow that to happen."

Cade caught the attention of Fourth Squad's commander. "Lyons, would you do the honors?"

"Yes sir," said the grizzled veteran. He bowed his head, waited a moment for the rest of the men in the room to do the same, and began to pray. "Lord, we are Your humble servants, ever mindful of our duty and obligations. Tonight we once again go into battle in Your name. Stand with us. Grant us the peace and protection afforded Your servants in such times of strife. I ask that You watch over every man that bears Your sword this night. Fill their hearts with courage and their souls with peace, and if it is their time to join You in heaven, welcome them into Your home with open arms. We ask this in the name of Your precious Son, Jesus Christ. Amen."

Cade addressed the group once more. "There will be a special Mass at sundown should any of you want to receive communion before going into battle. Immediately following the service, we'll meet on the grounds to board the choppers. Duncan, Riley, and Olsen, I need to speak to you. The rest of you are dismissed."

Once the room had cleared, Cade addressed his command team separately. "Recovering the Spear is our objective. Everything else, including the welfare of our men, is secondary to that. No matter what happens, we are going after the Spear, is that understood?"

The three men nodded.

"Olsen, I want you in a chopper overhead with a sniper rifle. Tell one of the Bravo snipers to do the same in another. Have him bring a spotter; Duncan will act as yours. Once the assault begins, you are free to pick and choose your targets. Concentrate on the Council members and anyone who appears to be attempting ritual magick. Warning shots are unnecessary."

"Right."

"Riley, you're with me. We're going in with First Squad as part of the ground unit. Once on the property, it will be our job to locate and retrieve the Spear."

"Got it, boss," said Riley, right on the heels of Duncan's, "Understood."

Cade dismissed them with a wave of his hand and turned back to study the maps for the fifth time that afternoon, wondering just what surprises the Necromancer, and possibly the Adversary, had in store for them.

* * *

After mass, Riley, Olsen, and Duncan walked to the armory, where Cade had been waiting for them. It was the team's habit of suiting up together and that day was no exception. They gathered in a small anteroom off the main chamber where the rest of Echo and Bravo Teams had assembled. First they pulled on a set of dark grey ceramic body armor that had been blessed by the Holy Father himself after its construction. Next were jumpsuits of black flame-retardant material that went over the body armor. In shoulder holsters, each man carried the standard issue HK Mark 23 .45 caliber handgun, complete with a twelve-round magazine, a flash suppressor, and a laser-targeting device. Two spare magazines for the pistols were affixed with Velcro to their left wrists. A combat knife was either affixed to their belts or in calf sheaths on the outside of their boots. Their swords, recently blessed again during Mass, were then slung across their backs, the hilt of the weapon extending just beyond their right shoulders for easy access. Lightweight Kevlar tactical helmets with built-in communications gear were worn on their heads.

Along with their pistols, each of the Knights also carried his weapons of choice.

For Riley, it was a Mossberg 590 12-gauge combat shotgun. He also carried a variety of plastic explosives and other detonation devices in the chest webbing he wore over his jumpsuit, in case they needed some demotion work during the assault.

Olsen had swapped his usual Barrett Light .50 caliber sniper rifle for something lighter. Stationed as he would be in the moving Blackhawk, the Barrett would be too awkward to use effectively, but a Marine-issue M40A3 would do the trick just fine. He also had a selection of throwing knives in a custom-made sheath strapped to his left arm between shoulder and elbow.

Cade and Duncan both carried HP MP5/10 submachine guns loaded with their trademark double magazines, giving them sixty rounds of available firepower before they'd need to reload.

Outside, the sound of the approaching Blackhawks pierced the quiet with the rhythmic thump of their rotors. Cade ordered the sergeants to get the loading started and followed them out into the fading afternoon sunlight just as the Blackhawks touched down on the lawn nearby.

The site of the nine choppers started Cade's blood pumping. This had always been the time he liked best, when the op was getting under way and he knew that soon he would once again be put to the test.

He was headed for what would probably be the most dangerous assignment the Order had ever given him, and yet he felt a sense of calm, of peace, a feeling that this was what he had been born to do.

He stepped up onto the Blackhawk's skid and signaled for the unit to get going.

As the chopper lifted into the air, the setting sun streamed out over the Lafayette commandery below him, and Cade found himself wondering idly if he would live to see its walls again.

Then, as the choppers turned as one to the west, Cade's thoughts turned to the details of the mission before him.

The time for questions was over.

It was time for action.

# CHAPTER 27

SIMON LOGAN STARED DOWN AT the weapon in the carrying case before him with a mixture of fear, awe, and barely suppressed elation.

The final raid on the Templar commandery had been a smashing success. His men had acted with more skill than he'd expected, taking several other key artifacts from the Templar vaults, an act that would be lavishly rewarded. The Spear had been secured in the special carrying case designed for just that purpose, the other items packed away in whatever materials they had at hand, and the assault team had escaped as quickly and as silently as they had arrived.

The traitor had played his role well.

And apparently, he'd been justly rewarded for his treachery. The Necromancer had not been unhappy to hear that Donaldson been trapped in the room's collapse as his men had made their exit.

It was one less pawn to be concerned about.

And now the legendary Spear of Longinus belonged to him.

Cautiously, the Necromancer reached out with one gnarled

hand and ran a finger along the Spear's shaft, a surge of power shooting up his arm. He'd been afraid the godly nature of the weapon would strike out against him and was pleased to discover his fears had been unfounded.

With considerably more confidence, he reached into the case, wrapped his fingers around the weapon, and pulled it free of the clasps that held it in place.

The Spear came to life.

Raw power flowed through the Necromancer, more power than he'd ever felt in his life. The grey haze through which he had begun to see the world was thrown back; vibrant colors and sounds assaulted his senses, as if a veil had been torn free, and he was seeing the world for the first time as it truly was. Possibilities unfolded before him, and he could see the righteousness of his path, knew beyond a shadow of a doubt that he was destined to hold this weapon in his hand, that it had traveled through the years just to arrive here, at this time, at this place, so that he might raise it up against his foes.

\* \* \*

The boats moved smoothly through the water under the powerful strokes of the oars. All the men were under noise discipline, but Cade realized that it really wasn't necessary. He could hardly hear the man next to him, never mind someone in one of the other boats, for all the din about them.

As darkness had settled, the swamp had come alive with sound.

The frogs had a chorus all their own, from the guttural belching of the bulls to the chirps of the smaller tree frogs. They were joined by the incessant buzz of the insects that swarmed around the Knights and the occasional hoot of a far-off owl, creating a cacophony that pressed against them on all sides.

From time to time a loud splash could be heard, and each time it was, the men in the boats tensed. They watched the water, wary of gators, but other than an occasional glimpse of something moving off in the distance, they didn't encounter any.

The going was slow; gator nests, currents, and submerged logs large enough to swamp their boats presented more than enough problems. Eventually their guide, a wizened old man who'd fished these parts for years and who believed he was leading law enforcement personnel on a drug raid, turned to Cade, and said, "Getting close. Ten, fifteen more minutes max."

Cade nodded his understanding and signaled the men.

Weapons were quickly checked, safeties taken off. The men shifted their positions slightly, preparing for the need to evacuate the boats quickly and silently.

Slowly, they closed on their destination. Up ahead, a light could be seen cutting through the trees.

As they emerged from a narrow channel into a wider passage, they came upon an incongruous sight. Rising out of the water was the statue of a stone cherub, its wings spread wide, smiling in frozen joy. A few feet away, a moss-covered Celtic cross also broke the surface. Several yards to their left, the remains of a small stone building could be seen on the nearby shore. The tall grass on either side gave glimpses of other forgotten monuments.

"What is this place?" Cade asked.

Their guide cast his gaze around uneasily. "It's what's left of the old Spanish mission. In the late-colonial days the local parish wouldn't let the unsaved be buried in town, so most of them were carted out here. Plots full of thieves and murderers and unbaptized infants. Some say the place is haunted."

"And you?" asked Cade.

The old man looked at him long and hard before answering. "I think there are things on this earth man ain't supposed to bother with. This place is one of them. Let's move along."

They continued forward and soon found themselves over the center of the submerged cemetery. A few markers rose above the surface, and as they steered between them, several other forgotten graves could be seen beneath the waterline.

Cade felt a sudden burst of power across his entire body, a sensation not unlike touching a live wire with his bare hand. It was so unexpected that he sat down abruptly, alarming those in the boat with him and forcing their guide to hold up his hand in the signal to stop.

The five boats coasted to a stop with Cade's boat in the lead and the others spread out behind it in an inverted V.

As the feeling faded, Cade gave himself a quick once-over, confirming that he was physically uninjured, but that didn't assuage the growing unease he felt. Riley asked if he was all right, but Cade ignored him for a moment, turning instead to gaze out into the growing darkness around them.

The cypress trees cast odd shadows across the water, their branches hanging down almost to the water's edge like mourners with their heads bowed. A breeze came up, causing the saw grass to sway lazily about. He saw no cause for alarm around them, however.

"I'm fine," he replied at last, deciding he'd wasted enough time. It was clear that whatever it had been, it was gone. "Get us moving again. I suddenly feel like a sitting duck."

Riley raised an arm and gave the signal for them to get under way.

That's when the trap was sprung.

Several forms surged out of the water around each boat, surprising the men inside them. Hands reached for the gunwales as the moss-covered faces of the corpses risen from the depths of the swamp screamed in silence at the men who faced them.

Cade didn't even have time to draw his sword as a revenant swarmed over the side right on top of him. He went down beneath its form, his hands locked about its throat in an effort to keep its teeth from sinking into his own neck. The creature pummeled him with its hands, its overgrown fingernails acting like claws as they slashed against his coveralls and armor.

The vessel farthest to the left was immediately overturned, the Knights inside disappearing into the murky water below. They would not resurface.

The others were more fortunate, the action from the men onboard preventing further mishaps.

But the attack was on in earnest.

As Cade struggled to keep the revenant from biting into his neck, Riley jumped to his defense. The master sergeant's boot shot forward and knocked the revenant's head clear of its body while his sword shot out and lopped off the hands of another revenant trying to climb inside their boat.

Around him, other Knights were fighting back, falling on the attacking revenants with their swords and combat knifes.

The battle was swift and deadly.

By the time the assault team had destroyed the last of the revenants, they had five casualties and three wounded Knights.

It was not an auspicious beginning.

Knowing time was running out, Cade regrouped his own team and got them headed toward the target again.

Three hundred yards later, they emerged from narrow, grassy channels into a wider lake-like area. Pulling out a pair of low-light binoculars, Cade surveyed their target. From here he could see that the bayou had taken to reclaiming the land on which the plantation house was built. The boathouse that had been prominent on the pictures from a few years ago was all but gone, with only its moss-shrouded peak still rising a few inches above the water. The swamp had not been content to stop there; almost a full third of the luxurious lawn had been swallowed up as well. It looked like Cade's men could run their boats right up onto the edge of the lawn instead of having to tie off at the docks as they had planned.

The soft glow of some kind of natural light, most probably candles or gas lanterns, could be seen in a few windows on the second floor. Otherwise, the plantation house and the surrounding grounds were dark.

Which was just as Cade had hoped.

"TOC to Olsen, TOC to Olsen."

Olsen, in the air inside one of the Blackhawks a few minutes away from the estate, answered the radio call immediately. "Go TOC."

"We've reached the edge of the grounds and are starting our advance. No resistance in sight. Wait five, then come in."

"Roger, TOC, Olsen out."

# CHAPTER 28

LOGAN STOOD IN WHAT WAS once the grand ballroom on the second floor of the decaying plantation house, looking out into the night through the open French doors. As always, he wore his hooded robe, his features all but lost in the shadows it created. Behind him, arrayed in a semicircle, were his six senior acolytes.

Together, they made up what was left of the famed Council of Nine.

*Or famed it will be*, the Necromancer thought, as he tightened his grip on the Spear of Longinus that he held in his right hand. *Now I have the power. Now I am invincible. Now is time for the world to know my name.*

But first he had to deal with the Templars.

And after that . . . after that there was still one more confrontation facing him.

"Their advance unit triggered the wards ten minutes ago," said his second-in-command. "We can expect the full force of their attack at any moment."

"Very well. Release the corpse hounds and prepare

yourselves for battle. I will call forth some special reinforcements and join you shortly."

"It is done."

One by one the acolytes filed out of the room, each with a specific task to perform. The Necromancer had known the Templars would come after them, he just hadn't believed they would find them so quickly. It had been less than six hours since his men had returned bearing their precious cargo; a problem in Tennessee had cost them several hours and had ended with six state troopers dead on the edge of some backwoods highway in the midst of the Cumberland Plateau. Still, six hours had been more than enough for him to call forth the power of the weapon now in his grasp. He knew that in time there would be so much more he could do, but for now, what little he had learned should be more than enough to deal with the damned Knights once and for all.

He stepped through the French doors and outside onto the small balcony just beyond. The night air was redolent with the smell of the swamp and the decay of the house around him. He breathed it in deeply, loving it. Death and decay; those were his partners, and he reveled in their presence.

He looked to the south, where a large thundercloud sat fat and heavy on the horizon.

*That will do nicely*, he thought with pleasure.

Raising his arms out to his sides he called out in a tongue long since dead to the world at large, a tongue he'd only just learned at the foot of his new benefactor.

From the tip of the Spear, lightning shot suddenly skyward.

In the distance, the storm turned toward him in response.

# CHAPTER 29

THE BLACKHAWKS CAME SWOOPING IN over the trees like avenging angels, hovering over the front lawn just long enough to dispatch their cargo; and then, with the exception of the lead two birds, they retreated back out over the swamps to wait until they were needed.

Olsen and Duncan were in the first of the two choppers that had stayed behind. They circled above the property, using the high-intensity spotlight mounted under the nose of the bird to highlight threats for the ground force and communicating with them via radio. From their vantage point they could see Cade and his men join up with Bravo Team. Fanning out, the group began its advance on the nearby buildings.

"Look!" Duncan cried, pointing.

The door to the plantation house opened, and several individuals stepped out into the porch. Duncan got a good look at them through the binoculars, and what he saw made his blood run cold. He'd seen those hooded robes before, worn by the sorcerers he and Cade had faced at Stone's; he knew what power they had at their disposal.

The battle was about to become bloody.

Olsen got on the radio to their commander. "Olsen to TOC."

"Go, Olsen," Cade's gruff voice replied.

"I count five hostiles on the porch, repeat five hostiles."

"Understood. Give the challenge, then engage at will."

Duncan was already waiting by the switch, and when Olsen gave him the signal, he tuned the choppers communication's system to broadcast externally.

His voice boomed out across the battlefield. "In the name of the Lord Almighty, I call upon you to relinquish your weapons and receive the mercy of Christ the King."

In response, one of the Council members raised his fingers to his lips. The men in the Blackhawk could not hear the resulting whistle over the sound of the rotors, but the men on the ground clearly did.

For a moment, nothing moved on the battlefield.

And then, in a thundering rush, dark forms came pouring out from around the sides of the house and headed straight for the Templar formation.

* * *

The first of the corpse hounds ran through an area of the lawn illuminated by the chopper's spotlight, and Duncan could hear the voice of the Bravo Team leader clearly over the radio in response. "What in the name of God?"

They were the size of Great Danes, but no living Dane ever looked like this. Their skin hung rotting on their frames, and their empty eye sockets seemed to blaze with an unholy light. They charged across the grounds with unnatural speed, moving unerringly toward the Knights who were advancing on the plantation house.

The Templars met the oncoming rush with brutal efficiency. They had positioned themselves in such a way as to deliver overlapping fields of fire, and their gunfire cut a swath through the enemy ranks.

Just as the Knights had discovered when fighting the revenants, these creatures were only minimally affected by the bullets that ripped through their already ravaged bodies. A few fell to lucky headshots, but the rest simply regained their feet or came on undeterred.

In seconds they would be among the Knights.

"Swords!" Cade called out over the communication's equipment and the men of both units drew their holy blades and met the oncoming charge straight on.

Swords flashed, hounds bayed, and both men and dogs bled into the night air.

High above, Olsen and the sniper in the other Blackhawk finally entered the fray.

They targeted the Council members still standing on the porch, taking out two of them with their first shots. Before the rest could respond to the threat, Olsen had fired again, striking a third. While he did not think the second shot had been a fatal one, at least there were two less sorcerers for them to worry about.

As the rest of the Council members dove out of sight behind the portico columns, Olsen turned his attention to the battle below him, seeking new targets, firing again and again until he was forced to reload.

The battle raged on.

In the distance, the storm gathered momentum.

* * *

Once he had secured control of the tempest, Logan set the second half of his plan into motion. Calling upon the power inherent in the Spear, and adding it to his own dark arts, he reached savagely across the barrier into a realm long since forgotten by most men.

With the aid of his magick, he swept up several of the realm's denizens and pulled them back into his side of reality. Controlling them, he sent the creatures forth, hidden in the heart of the storm.

* * *

Cade moved through the melee, Riley at his side. Grim determination was etched on his face as he moved, his blade flashing repeatedly in the moonlight. Each corpse brought him closer to the plantation house. The hounds were designed to slow them down, of that he was certain, and so he refused to give them what they wanted. With the core of Echo Team at his back, he smashed his way through the ranks of the enemy.

From out of the chaos in front of him charged an incredibly large beast; standing more than waist high, it resembled a full-grown lion more than a dog. Snarling, it launched itself at Cade.

As Riley watched, his commanding officer disappeared completely beneath the beast's form.

"Cade!" he cried, dispatching the corpse hound he was currently fighting and rushing over to his friend.

He needn't have worried; even as he looked on the point of Cade's sword came through the creature's skull from the inside out. With a mighty shove, the commander rolled the corpse off him, his sword still embedded to the hilt in the base of the creature's neck. Getting up, he placed a foot on the body and pulled the sword free.

Cade was covered with blood and other unrecognizable substances from the hound's corpse, but he was otherwise unhurt.

Riley clapped a hand on his shoulder in a silent show of support, and they turned to the battle once more.

A Blackhawk roared overhead, its light dancing across the lawn and over the front steps, and in its glow Cade saw a startling sight.

Gabrielle stood on the steps gesturing to him.

He raised his sword, to show he had seen her, and watched as she turned and disappeared inside the house.

It was clear that she wanted him to follow.

As chance, or providence, would have it, several quick shots from the helicopter above him cleared the last of the corpse hounds from his path.

The way to the steps was open.

"This way," he cried, charging forward, with Riley at his heels.

# CHAPTER 30

INSIDE THE PLANTATION HOUSE, THEY sheathed their swords and drew out their firearms. A double staircase immediately in front of them led up to the upper floors.

At the top stood Gabrielle, waiting.

Cade never hesitated.

He charged up the steps, with Riley close behind.

They encountered no one in the halls, so it was only a matter of moments before they found themselves led to the entrance to the grand ballroom on the second floor.

Across the room stood Logan, the Necromancer.

\* \* \*

"We've got trouble," Olsen said, inclining his head toward the window while he finished reloading his weapon.

Duncan turned to see what he was referring to and instantly wished he hadn't.

A thick bank of storm clouds had appeared practically out of nowhere, moving faster than any earthbound wind could have carried them. And through a break in the clouds, they caught sight of the cause of that speed within their depths; shapes writhed and rolled within the clouds, shapes that had no purpose for being on this God-given earth.

Clearly, they were some form of summoned being, but not one either Duncan, with his limited knowledge of such creatures, or Olsen, who'd faced more than his fair share, had ever seen before. They were a good ten to fifteen feet in length and shaped, more than anything else, like manatees, except instead of front fins they had fully functional arms complete with claws several inches in length. They had large bulbous heads with human faces and gaping maws full of oversized teeth.

*Their eyes*, thought Duncan in the instant before the spectres were upon them, *their eyes are full of hatred*.

* * *

Logan turned to face them as they entered the room. In his hand he held the Spear. He was dressed in a long, hooded robe, tied at the waist with a black sash. Cade recognized more than a few of the arcane symbols sewn onto its surface and knew that this was not a man to be trifled with.

But neither was he.

Riley moved out to his left, his weapon securely aimed at their foe, making it difficult for the sorcerer to strike them both with one blow.

The Necromancer, however, didn't even acknowledge his presence. His darkened hood concealed his features, but Cade could tell his gaze never wavered from him just the same.

"He said you would come."

The Necromancer's voice was distorted, garbled, and it took a moment for Cade to understand him. When he did, his words set his heart racing as the Templar Commander realized the necromancer could only be referring to one being.

*The Adversary.*

"Where is he?" Cade demanded.

Logan ignored the question, taking a step closer as he spoke. "Why are you here? Did you think you could defeat me?"

Cade raised his gun. "Put down the Spear. You will not be harmed if you do as you are told."

The Necromancer acted as if he hadn't heard. "You and your pathetic ally?" he asked, looking over at Riley for the first time. "Do you really believe you are strong enough to face me?"

He didn't wait for an answer. In a surprisingly lithe move, he swept the Spear around in an arc and pointed it at Riley.

Riley wasn't taking any chances. As soon as the Necromancer moved, he pulled his weapon's trigger.

Cade watched, stunned, as the bullets from Riley gun arced *around* the Necromancer and smashed harmlessly into the doors behind. Logan mouthed something in a tongue Cade could not recognize, and in the next instant Riley was lifted up off the ground and tossed halfway across the room.

The Templar sergeant slumped to the floor, unmoving.

Logan turned back toward Cade, returning the Spear to his side. With his other hand, he reached up and threw back his hood, revealing his features for the first time.

The right side of his face was a veritable ruin; his skin scarred from exposure to some kind of extreme heat, the flesh melted together and re-formed into some hideous approximation of normalcy. Like Cade's, his right eye had not escaped harm, but where Cade's was left intact as a milky white orb, the Necromancer's had been destroyed outright, leaving the empty socket to gape like an open wound in his face. A few remaining wisps of long white hair hung from his damaged scalp.

The similarities between Cade's condition and that of the necromancer were too obvious to ignore.

*Could this have been what the Adversary had intended for me?*

And then an even more disturbing thought.

*Why didn't he finish the job?*

Despite his inner turmoil, Cade kept his gun pointed in the Necromancer's direction. "Put down the Spear and step away from it," he said.

The Necromancer laughed. "Go ahead, shoot me," he said, spreading his arms wide, the Spear still held securely in his right hand. "You can't harm me and you know it. What I did to your companion was child's play. As long as I am in possession of *this*," - he shook the weapon slightly - "I am invincible."

Cade *did* know the rumors. He *had* heard the legends. He also knew that at least some of them regarding the Spear were true; he had seen the power of the weapon firsthand.

Yet he had little choice.

His enemy could not, *must not*, retain control of the Spear.

"This is your last chance, Logan. Put down the weapon."

The Necromancer smiled. Instead of obeying Cade's command, he began chanting under his breath. As he did so the head of the Spear started to glow a brilliant crimson in response.

* * *

The storm, and its fearsome passengers, hit them in a rush. One moment the helicopter was above the estate in clear skies, the next it was encased in a maelstrom of horrific proportions, surrounded by clouds so thick that if it weren't for the instruments, the pilots would have been unable to determine which direction was up. As it was they had their hands full, fighting against the gale force winds and struggling to keep the aircraft on station.

In the back, Duncan and Olsen, strapped into their seats with safety webbing and seat belts, did their best to keep the spectres away from the helicopter with shots from their weapons.

Their gunfire only had marginal effect, however. The bullets seemed to skip off the creatures' scaly hides or were tossed away in the winds before they could reach their targets.

Above the howl of the wind and the sharp clatter of their firearms, a new sound could suddenly be heard.

The sound of teeth tearing through metal somewhere in the rear of the aircraft.

Duncan looked at Olsen, and the same thought flashed in both their eyes.

*The engines.*

\* \* \*

Cade had no intention of letting his enemy call forth any more of his infernal allies.

He had to do something.

*But what?*

The necromancer was right; Cade couldn't harm him while he was in possession of the Spear.

*Couldn't harm him.*

But that didn't mean that Cade couldn't harm the Spear itself.

It was a difficult shot, made more so by the narrowness of the weapon's shaft and the room's dim lighting. It was a shot that few men could have made.

Cade was one of those men.

The shot flew true, striking the wooden shaft of the Spear a few inches below the metal shank that held the tip in place and splintering it into pieces. The head of the weapon flew off into the shadows behind the Necromancer, leaving him holding a useless shaft of oak.

Logan's shriek of pain and outrage echoed off the walls around them.

But before Cade could end the confrontation with another well-placed bullet, a tremendous blow shook the house, sending them all to the floor..

\* \* \*

A sharp whine filled the crew compartment, the sound cycling upward into almost painful levels; and then, with a loud crack, something snapped.

The Knights stared at the ceiling; the rotors had shut down.

Seconds later the loud braying of the emergency alarm filled their ears and the pilot gave the Mayday call over the radio.

As soon as he understood they were going down, Duncan pulled himself into a tight ball, protecting the back of his neck with his hands, just as he'd been taught.

One moment they were in the heart of the phantom clouds, the spectres feasting on their engines, and the next they were plummeting through the huge glass walls of the conservatory, the air filled with flying glass, crumpled steel, and the screams of the living and the dead as the ground came up to meet them.

\* \* \*

Cade pushed himself up on his hands just in time to see the Necromancer disappear through a door in the back of the room. Hauling himself to his feet, he looked for Riley, who was just climbing to his knees, a thin trickle of blood seeping across his forehead. Cade ran over to help him.

"Are you all right?" he asked, pulling the big man up by his arm.

Riley nodded, wiping at the blood absently. "Yeah, I'm fine. I could see and hear, I just couldn't move. What the hell just happened?"

"I don't know, and I don't have time to find out." He turned and pointed across the room. "Logan escaped through the back door. I want you to grab the the Spear and get out of the house with it. Do whatever you need to in order to keep it safe. I'm going after Logan."

"But . . ."

"There's no time. Get the Spear. I'll meet you out front as soon as I can."

And with that Cade ran off, following his enemy deeper into the house, leaving Riley to recover the artifact.

\* \* \*

Duncan came to with the straps of his seat belt cutting into his chest and threatening to suffocate him. He was hanging upside down in the darkness, bruised and battered, but intact.

He took a deep breath, gave a short prayer, and pressed the belt release with his left hand.

He landed on the ceiling of the Blackhawk with a jarring

crash. As he moved to get up, he put his hand in a pool of something thick and wet.

*Fuel oil*, was his first thought, but when he got a good whiff of the substance he corrected himself.

*Blood.*

The thought put more urgency in his movement.

Climbing carefully into a crouch, he reached into the leg pocket of his coveralls and withdrew one of the standard-issue light sticks he carried on every mission.

By its light he could see Olsen still hanging above him, held in place by his safety straps.

He could also see the wide stain on the front of the man's coveralls and the thick piece of shrapnel that had gone through them, his body armor, and, finally, deep into his chest.

With a tentative hand, he reached up to see if his companion was still alive.

# CHAPTER 31

L OGAN PLUNGED DOWN THE BACK steps and outside into the wall of fog he had summoned while on the run just moments before. With the loss of the Spear had come a loss of power, and he knew this latest act of sorcery wouldn't last very long. He had to be under cover before it disappeared

With a sense of direction bred from years of familiarity, he headed for the chapel.

He had to reach the Other before they caught up with him.

He would know what to do.

He would help him recover the Spear.

He had to.

To have come so far, only to lose it now would be unthinkable.

Logan couldn't understand what had gone wrong. His early-alarm system had worked perfectly, letting him know the assault was on its way. He'd placed his troops, summoned reinforcements the likes of which he had never been powerful enough to summon before, and had counterattacked before the

Templars had even known what was happening.

Yet somehow the damned Templars had managed to breach his defenses.

Everything he had worked for was in ruins.

From the sounds of the small-arms fire coming from other parts of the property, it seemed the Knights were still fighting against his allies, but he knew it wouldn't be long before the last of them were destroyed, and the full force of the Templar contingent would descend on the house.

He had to regain some measure of control before that happened.

Reaching the chapel, the Necromancer hauled the door open and stepped inside.

The chapel was lit with the same eerie red glow that always accompanied the Other's presence; but even as the Necromancer made his way down the center aisle, it slowly began to fade away until he was left standing before the altar alone in the darkness.

The Other had abandoned him for his failure.

\* \* \*

Cade emerged from the plantation house and stood for a moment on the back steps.

Ahead of him was a wall of grey. The fog was thick, unnatural. It felt more like a living presence than an inanimate object. He could sense it looming there, pressing against his awareness like an unseen danger, waiting to swallow him whole.

He knew that the Necromancer had disappeared into its depths.

He had no choice but to follow.

With his gun in one hand and his sword in the other, he plunged down the steps and into the mist.

\* \* \*

Unable to free Olsen from the twisted webbing that held him in place, Duncan was forced to support Olsen's body with one hand and slice through the webbing and seat belt with his combat knife.

He caught his companion's body as it dropped and carefully hauled him out of the wreckage of the chopper. He found a relatively clear piece of floor and laid him gently down upon it. Now that he was free of the crew cabin he could see that the chopper had smashed through ceiling of the conservatory and buried itself in the wall that attached it to the plantation house.

Looking through the gaping hole they had created, he could see the raging storm. Lightning flashed, illuminating the strange shapes moving in the clouds, but for the moment they no longer seemed interested in the wreck of the chopper.

Which was just fine by him.

A quick look at the front of the Blackhawk let him know there was no chance that either of the pilots had survived, so he returned to Olsen's side, only to find him conscious.

Olsen's hand reached out to Duncan.

"It's all right. You're okay," Duncan said softly, kneeling over his companion and doing what he could to block his view of the large hunk of glass protruding from the man's chest.

Olsen tried to respond, but only managed to cough up a large mass of blood.

It was clear to Duncan that his companion didn't have long to live.

A man lay dying, and he had the power to save him, power that had been given to him by the Lord above. To ignore that power, to pretend it didn't exist simply because he didn't understand it was not honoring the Lord, as he'd believed for so long, but denying Him. Cade had it right, Duncan realized. It wasn't where the power came from, but how it was used that was important.

He made his decision.

"Listen to me, Nick. I'm going to remove the piece of glass from your chest and see what I can do about that wound. It's not going to be easy. You've got to stay with me, fight to stay alive, do you hear me?"

Olsen stared at him glassy-eyed, and Duncan was afraid he was already past the point of understanding, but finally he gave a short nod.

"All right. On the count of three." Duncan grasped wrapped his hands around the shard of glass. He made certain he had a good grip on it, ignoring the way it bit into the flesh of his hands. He could deal with that later, after he managed to stabilize Olsen.

He caught Olsen's gaze. "One, two, three . . ."

He pulled.

Olsen screamed.

The shard of glass came free with a wet, sucking sound.

The blood flowed in waves.

Duncan brought his own bleeding hands over the massive wound in Olsen's chest.

* * *

Cade did his best to move forward in a straight line, trusting that his sense of direction wouldn't fail him.

Yet within moments, he knew he had sadly underestimated the fog. It felt like a cocoon. Visibility was limited to less than a foot in front of his face, the thickness of the fog working to strip his sense of direction from him.

He slowed, then stopped. He wanted to use his Sight, but there were too many unearthly creatures roaming the grounds at the moment; his Sight would be like a beacon fire in the night for them. Walking in the stuff was bad enough. Fighting a pitched battle against barely visible opponents would be far worse.

No, he had no choice but to continue forward.

He stepped off again, moving cautiously, aware of the passage of each moment like a ticking bomb, knowing every second increased the possibility that Logan had diverged from this course.

A shape moved in the fog ahead of him, a suggestion of a hooded figure, and Cade surged ahead, trying to catch up.

Ten steps later he emerged from the fog entirely.

The moon shone brightly, just as it had at the start of the incursion.

By its light he could see that the figure he was chasing was Gabrielle. As he watched, she disappeared inside the oak door of a small chapel.

\* \* \*

The Necromancer fell to his knees, pleading. "No! Don't go! You can defeat them. You can recover the Spear, we can still succeed!"

His words bounced off the nearby walls, mocking him with their echo and the emptiness of the chapel around him.

He could feel his power waning; whatever gifts the Other had provided were disappearing along with their provider, and he was being left with only the petty knowledge he had gained on his own in the years before the Other's coming.

His dreams of glory were fading with each passing second.

A shout from outside reached his ears.

He had only moments before his enemy was upon him.

He looked around frantically for a weapon.

* * *

Cade pushed the door open fully, letting the moonlight illuminate the aisle before him that led into the heart of the chapel.

He could see an altar in the shadows ahead, but no sign of Gabrielle.

"Gabbi?" he called.

When no answer came, he stepped inside, waiting a moment on the other side of the threshold to let his eyes adjust to the dim light.

Cautiously, he started down the center aisle toward the altar.

Halfway to his destination, the quiet of the small chapel was broken.

Shrieking, the Necromancer charged out of the shadows and swung a large metal candleholder at Cade's head.

Cade ducked beneath the attack, allowing the makeshift club to pass harmlessly over his head. Adrenaline surging, Cade went on the offensive, stepping inside his enemy's swing, one hand against the other man's upper arm, preventing him from coming back in that direction with another attack. At the same time, Cade's left fist hammered into the Necromancer's midsection,

Joseph Nassise

once, twice, three times.

His enemy countered by continuing his turn and coming around full circle, the heavy base of the candleholder sweeping in at foot level.

Cade jumped up and over the weapon, only to catch the other end across the side of his face as the Necromancer deftly maneuvered it to continue his assault.

The blow sent Cade to the ground, his sword tumbling out of reach.

The Necromancer rushed in, shoving the base of the candleholder at Cade's face, intending to end the confrontation with one well-placed blow.

The Templar Commander would not be silenced that quickly.

He threw himself backward, into one of the pews, avoiding the potentially lethal blow as the base of the weapon smashed into the end of the pew itself.

The Necromancer screamed in frustration and lifted the heavy weapon over his head for another strike.

That was all Cade needed to turn the tide in his favor.

Diving out of the pew, Cade struck him hard, driving his shoulder into his solar plexus in a makeshift tackle. His momentum carried them across the aisle and against the end of the row of pews on the other side, where the Necromancer smashed bodily into the unyielding surface.

The pain of the blow forced him to drop the candleholder.

Gripping his robes with one hand, Cade rained several blows down on the necromancer's unprotected face.

A knife appeared from somewhere inside the Necromancer's robes, and he slashed at Cade with it.

A sliver of moonlight danced along its edge as it came inward toward him, giving Cade enough warning to skip to the side, out

244

of the way of its razor edge.

The move forced him to let go of his hold on the other man's robes.

Knowing he needed more room if he was to evade further attacks, Cade stepped out into the open area in front of the altar. Logan rushed him.

Cade waited, timing his action.

As the knife came in, he stepped inside its reach, smashing the hard edge of both hands against the inside of the other man's forearm. Keeping his left hand on his attacker's wrist, pinning the blade away from him, he used the ridge of his other hand in the opposite direction to strike the Necromancer hard along the line of his neck, just below the ear.

The blow achieved its desired effect, stunning his attacker

Securing a two-handed grip on the other man's already extended arm, Cade stepped forward and heaved him bodily over his shoulder, throwing him to the floor on the edge of the altar steps.

Cade quickly recovered his sword and stalked back to where the Necromancer lay cowering on the steps of the altar.

Staring down at his foe, weapon in hand, he felt his rage spiral out of control.

*This is the man who masterminded the attacks against the Order.*

*This is the man who was responsible for the death of over 100 of his brethren.*

*This is the man who had cooperated with the Adversary.*

That last thought was enough to shatter what little control Cade had left. The man deserved to die.

With a cry of rage, Cade raised his sword over his head and brought it whistling down toward the Necromancer's quivering form.

As the sword fell, a shout rang out from elsewhere in the room.

"Stop!"

The voice, and its tone, was instantly recognizable to Cade.

He twisted slightly and managed to turn the blade aside in time to prevent skewering the defeated man before him. Instead of slashing through the Necromancer, the blade struck harmlessly off the carpet next to him. The defeated man buried his face in his hands and mewled in fear.

Cade barely noticed.

He had eyes only for his dead wife, who was standing a few feet behind the altar.

"You need him, Cade."

He snorted. "Like hell I do. The world will be a better place without him." His thoughts turned for a brief moment to the death toll that could be laid at this man's feet. "Justice demands his death."

"Then justice will have to take a backseat. You will need him at some point in the future. I can see it. Without him, your vengeance will go unclaimed."

Cade considered her remarks, knowing as he did so that if it hadn't been for her previous warning, they might never have known about the traitor within their ranks. But still he wanted to know more,

"What will I need him for? And when?"

"I don't know."

"You don't know, or you can't say?"

She didn't respond.

Motion at the door caught his attention. Several Knights entered the chapel, their weapons at the ready.

"Sir?" Riley called, the question in his voice obvious.

"Here," Cade replied, looking toward them with the briefest of glances. "The room's secure."

He turned back to face his wife, only to find she had gone as suddenly and as mysteriously as she had come.

But she had accomplished her end.

The Necromancer would live, at least for the time being. Others in the Order would turn their skills upon him and eventually he would tell them all he knew. At that point his fate would be up to those in charge.

But for the moment, he would live.

Cade turned his defeated prisoner over to his second-in-command and watched as the man was searched and secured by the other soldiers. Riley himself filled him in on what was happening.

"The complex is under control. The last of the Council members have been rounded up. A few of them are even talking, and with their help we hope to have the rest of the missing artifacts rounded up before long."

"Casualties?"

"Eighteen dead, twelve wounded." Riley hesitated, obviously searching for words.

"Just say it," Cade said gruffly, a sudden dread filling his heart.

"The chopper Olsen and Duncan were in went down. Smashed straight into the conservatory. Olsen took a piece of shrapnel deep in the chest."

"Is he dead?"

"No, boss. And that's the problem. By all rights he should be, yet it looks like he's going to be all right. Whatever Duncan did when he pulled him out of the wreckage saved his life. Some of the men are calling it a miracle."

Cade covered his surprise. "Let them call it what they want," Cade said gruffly. "Just make sure Olsen gets what he needs."

"Yes, sir."

As Riley turned away, Cade reached out and grabbed his arm. "Keep Duncan close, just in case."

Riley grinned. "You can count on it, sir."

As Riley escorted the prisoner out of the chapel, Cade remained behind. He walked down the center aisle and took a seat in the first row of pews, facing the altar.

"Gabbi? Are you still here?"

Only the silence answered him.

Using his Sight, he tried to find some trace of her lingering on the other side.

Where in the living world the chapel had lost its glory and had become just a small dark corner in a larger, darker world, in the Beyond, a startling transformation was taking place. Even as he watched, a golden light blossomed in the center of the room, slowly driving away the darkness and the shadows until it shone with the faith that had once infused its walls, a faith that was slowly forcing its way back in. The room was empty, but it was not without power.

And in that moment, his heart echoed that brilliance.

He found himself hoping that one day the burden of vengeance would be lifted from him as well, and that he, too, could feel such a cleansing.

But for the time being, he had a vow that still needed to be fulfilled.

Turning off his Sight and returning to the real world, he took one last look around.

The chapel seemed empty, but deep inside he knew the truth.

After all these years, he'd been so close.

Raising his head, he stared into the shadows at the back of the room.

"Run," he said softly. "Run while you can. One day I will find you, and on that day there will be a reckoning."

He hefted his sword and stared at the word etched into its blade. "A reckoning, indeed."

With that he turned away and walked back up the aisle and into the rising dawn outside.

Made in the USA
San Bernardino, CA
23 December 2012